Laura is suffering from total amnesia caused by a catalepsy. Facing people who are absolutely unknown to her, she is amazed to learn that one improbable character is her husband, and that another is a senior police officer; and even Laura's buoyant spirits quail when she is told the circumstances in which she was discovered – clutching a carving knife in the kitchen of her country house (Royalties – she learns she is a successful writer) which is drenched in human blood. She learns too that there is no corpse.

Laura discovers a lot of other things about her past, knowledge that would have led many other women to prefer the cataleptic state. But she is made of sterner stuff, and her very active mind begins to ask itself what *could* have happened.

Then bits of memory start to come back – though nothing relating to the terrible night.

This is a clever and complicated suspense novel, with a strong detective element and an excellent setting in the West Country of England. It strikes the particular note of originality for which George Baxt is celebrated (most notably in *A Queer Kind of Death*) and combines it with a powerful and puzzling plot.

We are very pleased to welcome George Baxt to our list.

D1339733

By the same author

# The Affair at Royalties

## GEORGE BAXT

MACMILLAN

SBN Boards: 333 12649 1

*First published 1971 by*
MACMILLAN LONDON LTD
*London and Basingstoke*
*Associated companies in New York Toronto*
*Dublin Melbourne Johannesburg & Madras*

*Printed in Great Britain by*
RICHARD CLAY (THE CHAUCER PRESS), LTD.,
*Bungay, Suffolk*

For Harold Schiff
who could use some dedication

# Chapter One

Perhaps my eyelids are pasted together, she thought to herself, or sealed with the wax used by undertakers. Then I'm embalmed, which can't be the case because I can feel my temples throbbing, my heart pounding and I'm positive I just heard somebody clear their throat. If it wasn't somebody clearing their throat then it was the distant rumble of a truck on the street, and if I can hear a distant rumble then my ears are in good shape and unsealed. No, I am definitely not embalmed. If I'm not dead, why can't I open my eyes?

She concentrated harder on opening her eyes, her brows furrowing in frustration, recalling, as only the subconscious can suddenly help one recall, being presented at the age of three with a set of blocks and wondering whether to stack them, strew them or fling them about, thereby establishing a reputation.

Open, damn you, she silently commanded, but the stubborn resistance continued. She felt herself on the verge of being engulfed by a wave of fear and fought to resist the accompanying panic. Control, she said to herself, control. This is no worse than fending off a pass from an unattractive man. Laugh gaily and flick some cigarette ash in his face, except there was no laughter in her and she was aching for a cigarette.

'Laura.'

How softly and gently the name was spoken. Was it the throat-clearer who dropped the name, or had she imagined it was spoken?

Laura.

Her brows unfurrowed, the eyelids stopped fluttering and her face recomposed into concentration. Now who is Laura and what is she?

'Her fingers are moving.' It was a woman who spoke.

So there's two of them. Good, there's safety in numbers. *Her fingers are moving.* Whoever she is, she spoke those four words with the sort of underlined triumph I always imagined Marie Curie spoke when she announced to her husband, 'Sweetie, we've discovered radium.' What's the big deal about my moving my fingers?

*Dear God.* A new and more frightening supposition worried her. Have I been paralysed? Is that it? Is that why I can't move my eyelids, is that why *she* is so thrilled by the movement in my fingers. But I've never known paralysis to attack eyelids. Every paralysed victim in books or movies can blink their eyelids, blink once if you mean 'no', blink twice if you mean 'yes', and three if by land. No, that's one if by land if it's Paul Revere suddenly galloping alongside my train of thought.

Fingers. All right, she thought with fresh determination, I'll make those little digits get to work for me. Now let me think, what is this I feel (and whoever you two are don't tell me, let me discover for *myself*). It's linen. It's starched linen. Ah! It's a bedsheet. Now that's established, where do I go from here? A bedsheet is a vast expanse and I can't explore that for the rest of the day (maybe it's night. *Maybe it's the moon over Cornwall* . . .).

'She's humming!' It's the woman again and by God she's right, I *am* humming. It's progress to say the least. Time out for an inventory. I can hear. I can feel and my vocal chords are in order. What's with the eyelids?

'Laura, it's Arthur.'

Miller? But I don't know Arthur Miller. Then she reminded herself. Oh yes, I met him once briefly at a cocktail party in Easthampton and it was 'How do you do' and 'So nice to meet you' and . . . what in God's name *is* all this? Who needs Arthur Miller at a time like this? I am lying in bed, undoubtedly miraculously recovering from a near-fatal illness, but brought on by what?

Near-fatal illness. Why not near-fatal accident? Why not

8

near-fatal marriage? I've known many a husband and wife near-paralysed by marriage, and why think of that *now*?

'She's groaning,' she heard the woman say.

'She sometimes talks in her sleep,' she heard the man reply.

'Doctor, should I give her another hypo?'

'No, I think she's coming out of it.'

That was a new voice, she realised. So there's three of them. There's the Laura hunter, like that poor slob sloshing through the swamps of Louisiana crying for Chloe, there's the lady who's apparently documenting me for posterity ('Her fingers are moving,' 'She's humming,' etcetera) and a doctor.

She found 'Doctor' somewhat comforting and 'another hypo' somewhat disturbing.

*I think she's coming out of it.*

Where have I been? *I've been to London to see the Queen.*

'She's giggling.'

Lady, she now thought, whoever you are, don't ever sit across from me at a dinner table. 'She's lifting her fork. It's poised over the salad. She's spearing a tomato. It's moving towards her mouth. Tomato now twelve o'clock high. Her lips are parted. Her mouth is open. Tomato entering mouth. Tomato planting flag on tongue.'

She sighed and then waited. She gave it another few seconds, but the sigh wasn't documented and she now had a sinking feeling they were growing bored with her. Perhaps, she thought anew, perhaps I should go back to the eyelids.

'I think the light's bothering her.' That was probably the Doctor. 'Lower the shade a bit.'

She heard a slight rustling noise, then soft footsteps followed by the sound of a windowshade lowering. Then more rustling, more footsteps, and the Doctor said, 'Thank you, Miss Murdock.'

She thought hard. Miss Murdock. Do I know a Miss Murdock? Not 'Thank you, nurse' or 'Thank you, sister'

9

depending on what country I'm in. Country. Hell that's the least of my worries. I know I'm in bed, but where? Hospital? Sanatorium? Hotel? Home?

Where's home?

A dozen thoughts began to weave themselves into an unpleasant pattern. What's wrong with me? Where am I? 'What's my name?'

'She spoke!'

Oh, good for you, Miss Murdock. If there's a Pulitzer Prize for observation you deserve it hands down.

Slowly her eyelids parted and with difficulty she attempted to focus. If this is a television set, she thought, where's the fine tuner? I see three blurs and for all I know it's ectoplasm. Well at least I can speak ('*She spoke!*') and my eyelids are *not* glued together and I'm positively alive so I'm ahead.

'Laura, Laura my darling.'

The way he said that, she thought, it's almost touching. Laura my darling. Whoever Laura is she'd better speak up and make her presence known. This guy sounds as though he loves his Laura and Laura might be a lucky girl.

She reserved the final decision on how lucky Laura might be until she got a better look at him. He might be short, pock-marked and bald with the extra added attraction of yellowing fangs in which case Laura was well out of it. She blinked her eyes, furiously irritated at their lack of focus.

'I can't focus!' she heard herself shout.

'Relax, relax.' The balm was flowing from the Doctor's mouth. Whatever it is, Doctor, she mused, you ought to patent and bottle it. 'The optic nerves are delicate threads. In a few seconds they'll readjust and your vision will return to normal.'

'You're a blur,' she said with the severity of the Red Queen in *Alice In Wonderland*.

'Be patient, we'll soon come into focus.'

'And then what?'

'And then you'll be able to see us,' said the Doctor.

She couldn't refute that statement.

'There's three of you.'

'That's right!' chirped Nurse Murdock.

'Who are you?'

'I'm Elaine Murdock. I'm your private nurse.'

*Private* nurse. Somebody's got money.

'And I'm Emory ... Emory Flint ... *Doctor* Flint ... don't you recognise my voice?'

She said nothing. She didn't dare. She didn't recognise the voice.

'Laura.' It was old sexy again. 'Don't you recognise *my* voice.'

She didn't give a damn about his voice. She was wondering why he was calling her Laura.

'Why do you call me Laura?' Her voice was sharp and she was annoyed. The other three exchanged glances, the Doctor's and Arthur's holding until the Doctor shook his head sadly. 'Why do you call me Laura?' she insisted. Before anyone could answer, she heard a door open, footsteps, the door shut and the footsteps advanced. A fourth blur appeared.

'How is she?' She liked this voice. It was deeply resonant and cultured. She heard whispering and she didn't like that one bit.

'Stop that whispering! Who are you? *You!* Number Four!' Having said it, she was forced to suppress a giggle. She sounded to herself like an arch-villainess in a science-fiction film.

'We've never met before,' said Number Four.

'You're English,' she said. 'I can tell by your accent. As a matter of fact ...' She stopped in mid-sentence. They were *all* English. She voiced it. 'You're *all* English!' For want of anything better to say she added, 'Why are you all English?'

'You're in London,' said Number Four.

'That explains it,' she said contentedly, again blinking her eyes furiously.

'What's wrong with her eyes?' she heard Number Four ask, followed by more whispering.

'My name is not Laura!' she said in an explosion. A momentary silence was broken by Number Four.

'Who are you?' he asked.

'I'm not Laura,' she said stubbornly. 'I hate that name.'

'What name would you prefer?' It was still Number Four. The others didn't mind his sudden domination, or didn't seem to, and she wondered about that.

'You're very inquisitive,' she said. 'Are you a policeman?' More silence.

'Well *are* you?' She couldn't steady her trembling voice.

'Why would I be a policeman?'

'Well for one thing, the others have let you take over.'

'Well, well, well,' the twinkle in his voice not escaping her, 'at least you haven't lost your powers of deduction.'

His comment stopped her for a moment. *My* powers of deduction. She tried to force her brain to work harder. *My* powers of deduction. She inquired in a timid voice, 'Am I Agatha Christie?'

'You're getting warmer!' chirped Miss Murdock.

'I *loathe* games.'

'You're Laura Denning,' said Number Four briskly.

Laura Denning. *Impossible!*

'I can't be Laura Denning.' She felt there was enough conviction in her voice to sway a jury.

'Why not?' Number Four was treating her like a child and she didn't like it one bit. Whoever she was, she couldn't stand condescension, and his voice was highly seasoned with it.

'Don't treat me like a child, Number Four.' He started to remonstrate, but she would not allow herself to be interrupted. 'I can't be Laura Denning because I don't feel like Laura Denning whether I have or have not lost my so-called powers of deduction. But I tell you this, I have intuition and my intuition tells me no good is going to come of *any* of this! Now let's begin at the beginning and you

12

play the game *my* way or we don't play at all!'

She didn't hear Arthur interject under his breath, 'That's Laura.'

'Nurse Murdock,' she said with admirable authority, 'these questions are directed at you. Are you there?'

Nurse Murdock moved closer to the bed. 'I'm right here.'

'Is this a hospital?'

'It's a private sanatorium.' Number Four whispered in Nurse Murdock's ear rapidly as the next question was aimed and fired.

'How long have I been here?'

Nurse Murdock looked at Number Four who nodded.

'Three weeks.'

*Three weeks.*

'Why was I brought here?' Number Four nodded again to the nurse.

'You were suffering from shock.'

'Shock?' She was shocked. 'You mean shell-shock? Is this wartime England?'

'Good heavens no,' said Nurse Murdock, 'that was years ago.'

Years ago. *Years ago.* 'You mean I'm middle-aged?'

'You're thirtyish.'

That came as a relief. As a patient, she knew she was in trouble, but as a woman she still had a fighting chance.

'What sort of shock landed me here?'

Doctor Flint rescued Nurse Murdock. 'It was an emotional upset, Laura.'

She fought to keep her fists from clenching and her lips from twitching. She did not want them to think her on the verge of a relapse. She desperately wanted confirmation of what she thought was the most obvious, 'Am I suffering a nervous breakdown?' but her instincts warned her to hold the question in reserve. One thought kept chipping away at her mind like a sculptor attacking a fresh block of marble, was she the victim of some sort of conspiracy, and if so,

13

why? She was pleased with herself at the coolness and crispness of her next question.

'Am I free to leave anytime I choose?'

Nurse Murdock jockeyed back into position. 'As soon as Doctor says you're fully recovered.'

'And when will that be?'

Doctor Flint spoke up briskly. 'When I decide you're physically fit.'

He means mentally fit, she thought to herself. He doesn't say that because he thinks it might send me back into shock again. Doctors can be very devious. She decided to call his bluff.

'You mean mentally fit.'

'Shock can also confuse the mental faculties,' said the Doctor.

*Maybe it's the moon over Cornwall. . . .*

'She's humming again,' said Nurse Murdock.

'She always hums when she's thinking.' That was Arthur.

Do I really? He sounds so positive. He was right on the nose too. I *am* thinking. I'm thinking why are they avoiding stating the obvious. When he identified himself as Arthur, I immediately associated him with the playwright I'd met briefly in Easthampton some years ago. Easthampton is a summer resort in Long Island. Long Island is part of New York and that's in America. Lots of writers and publishers own or rent summer homes in Easthampton. Maybe if I polished this tiny memory, from under the coat of rust might emerge my name. She realised she was fidgeting with the bedsheets and felt like slapping her fingers but didn't.

'Why have you brought me to England?'

Arthur rubbed his chin and waited for a sign from either the Doctor or Number Four. Nurse Murdock folded her hands and cocked her head towards Number Four. Number Four nodded at Arthur.

Arthur said with a faint croak in his voice, like a shy frog paying court, 'You've lived here for over eight years.'

She felt her eyes tear up, further confusing the process of

14

focusing as her voice detonated. 'Damn you people! Why hasn't one of you said it? I have amnesia! You could bloody well tag me with any number of identities! You ... Flint ... Doctor Flint ... if you *are* a Doctor ...' she thought she heard a quick intake of breath, 'why don't you honestly state the facts of my condition? Was I hit over the head or something? And if so, *why*? How long does this amnesia last? And who wrote this scene anyway? *Kafka?*'

Doctor Flint chuckled and then said with enthusiasm, 'That's the fight I've been looking for!'

'Full marks for me! Who's got a handkerchief?' Nurse Murdock came to the rescue with a tissue and the patient dabbed at her eyes as Doctor Flint made some attempt at an explanation, ignoring Number Four's urgent signal for a consultation.

She listened with the patience and concentration of a young wife receiving an introduction to Cordon Bleu cookery. She began to trust the man as he spoke.

'We've known each other for close to seven years, Laura.'

'Why don't I recognise your voice?'

'For the same reason you don't recognise Arthur's or acknowledge you are Laura Denning. You *are* suffering from amnesia, but I am convinced it is only a temporary condition. This is not unusual in cases of extreme shock.'

'Like a soldier in battle.'

'That's right,' he said warmly. She felt very brave.

'What was the shock?'

'We hope eventually you'll be able to tell us.'

I'll be damned, she thought, I'll really be damned. 'You say I'm suffering shock, yet you don't know *why*?'

'That's right.'

'Where was I at the time?'

'You were staying at Royalties.'

She wondered if that was a town or a girlfriend's house. Doctor Flint seemed to have read her mind.

'That's your cottage in Harborford.'

Harborford. Cornwall. A fishing village. A cliff. Rocks.

15

A path to the beach. A steep path. A dangerous one. A dangerous game. *Associations*. Harborford's the right button, Doctor. Keep pressing. The memory door might open.

'Tell me more about Harborford, Doctor. Why was I there? How long have I owned this cottage?'

'My poor Laura.' That was Arthur who spoke, and though he spoke the words tenderly, they made her feel like a basket case.

'Please . . .' she fought to speak the name and won the battle, '. . . Arthur. This conversation is restricted to doctor and patient. Doctor?'

'You purchased the cottage some three years ago, with the royalties from your superb book on Jack the Ripper.'

'*Beyond a Black Veil.*'

'She remembers!' cried Arthur.

'Be quiet, Arthur!' The rebuke brought a flush to his face and he fumbled in his jacket pocket for a cigarette. 'It almost won Laura Denning a Pulitzer Prize, didn't it, Doctor?'

'Yes, Laura.'

'Really, Arthur, any well-read person knows that book, whether they've read it or not, so there.' She realised immediately she must sound to them like a spoiled, petulant child, but she justified her attitude to herself with the special nature of her situation. 'Royalties is the name of the cottage and there I was at Royalties in a state of shock. Who found me?'

'Arthur found you,' said the Doctor. There was apparently no escaping Arthur unless by a divine judgement of God, and then she gasped.

'Oh dear. Oh, poor Arthur. Are you my *husband*?'

'Of course I am, darling.'

For want of anything better to say under her hazy circumstances, she inquired sweetly, 'How've you been, Arthur?'

'Frantic with worry over you, darling.' She heard him

16

move forward and then she felt his hand close tightly over hers. After what she hoped was a proper few moments, she moved her hand away.

'How old am I, Arthur?'

He spoke suavely and with humour. 'If I spoke the truth, you'd file for divorce.' There was the kind of laughter that made her wonder if cocktail orders would now be taken.

'Doctor?'

'Yes, dear.'

'Let's get back to the cottage. Arthur has found me. Would you elaborate on that please?' Arthur took a deep drag on his cigarette as the Doctor complied.

'It was shortly after two p.m., three weeks ago last Monday.'

'What's today?'

'Thursday.'

'Please continue.'

'You were seated at the kitchen table. The kitchen is at the rear of the cottage, the cliff side. Your eyes were open, but unseeing. You had suffered the complete loss of your senses and your feelings.'

*Have you lost your senses? Have you no feelings?* (Who had said that to her? She was positive she had heard a man speak those words. Arthur?)

The doctor had continued speaking through her thoughts. 'Arthur summoned Doctor Kettering in the village. He correctly diagnosed catalepsy and recommended immediate hospitalisation. Arthur reached me in London. I came as quickly as I could, and the following morning you were moved here. Now,' she thought she heard him rubbing his hands together, 'we can start probing for the cause of the shock.'

'Doctor.' The word fell like a rubber stamp on an official document. 'Let's put a little flesh on the skeleton.' She struggled to a sitting position and with Nurse Murdock's help was soon propped against two pillows. No one spoke during the procedure, but her senses told her there had been an exchange of covert looks. She was beginning to enjoy the situation immensely.

'Comfortable?' asked Nurse Murdock.

'Physically, yes. Thank you. Doctor Flint, what was the state of the kitchen when I was found?'

The Doctor looked at Arthur. Arthur looked at Number Four who was chewing on an unlit pipe.

'Tell her,' said Number Four. Arthur took another drag on his cigarette and then stubbed it out in an ashtray on the night table. Meantime, she wondered whether to tell them, I can see you clearly now. My vision has cleared and it's sharp and bright and I don't recognise any of you. Her decision was split-second. She would tell them nothing. She would play-act at continued fuzziness. Instinct told her to remain silent. The tall, somewhat distinguished looking man with black hair, grey temples, startling blue eyes with a trace of bagginess beneath them, horn-rimmed glasses, well-proportioned body and strong, faintly hairy fingers stubbing out a cigarette in the ashtray at her right elbow was about to speak.

'When I came into the kitchen, you were seated at the table staring, I thought, at me.' Hello, Arthur. 'I spoke your name several times before I realised you were ... ill. The table was set for lunch.'

'How many settings?'

'Two.'

'Was there food on the stove or in the oven?'

'There was a bowl of sea food salad on the table.'

She folded her hands somewhat primly. 'Was there any sign of a struggle in the room? Overturned chair, broken crockery, anything like that?' Out of the corner of one eye, she thought she caught a look of admiration on the face of the middle-aged gentleman chewing an unlit pipe. If that's a habit, she thought briefly, you have badly chipped teeth.

'Yes,' said Arthur solemnly, 'there had been a struggle. Two chairs were overturned, there were broken dishes on the floor ...'

18

'What about me?'

'What do you mean?'

'Did I look as though I might have taken part in this struggle? You know,' she couldn't resist adding, 'as though I might have been fighting off rape or something equally titillating?'

'Yes, you did.' His voice was trembling and he shot a look at the pipe clencher. That, she decided, was Number Four. The short, pudgy, bald-headed man with the paunch standing behind Arthur was undoubtedly Doctor Flint.

'We've come this far, Mr Denning,' said Number Four, 'you might just as well tell her the rest.'

Nurse, she couldn't help thinking, stand by for a hypo.

Arthur sat on the bed and took her hand. She made no effort to remove hers. Here was one chain she had no intention of breaking. She wanted to hear it all and the devil take the hindmost. He spoke rapidly, anxious to be rid of the words as though each was tainted and infected.

'Your hair was dishevelled. Your dress was torn at the shoulder. There were three scratches on your left cheek . . . they're almost gone now.' She closed her eyes as she felt the blood draining from her face.

'Tell me the rest,' she managed to say.

'Damn it, I can't!'

Her eyes flew open. 'Tell me! If it's *that* bad maybe it'll shock me back to reality and hooray for us! *Tell me!*'

He withdrew his hand and stood up staring down at her. 'There was blood on your dress, on the table, on the floor and on the wall near the stove.'

'What about a weapon?' She didn't sound like herself, whoever she was.

'There was a carving knife. The blade was caked with blood.'

'Where was the knife? On the floor? The table?'

'You were clenching it tightly in your right hand.'

Chapter Two

This, thought Number Four, could be the sleep-walking scene from *Macbeth*, except the protagonist is wide awake and completely aware of surroundings and situation. The patient was gently tapping the palm of her right hand with her left index finger, and humming to herself. She might have been sitting under a hair-drier. He realised there were several things to admire in her, in addition to her physical attractiveness.

Her amazing composure after hearing she might be a murderess, her pugnacious attitude towards Arthur Denning as she forced the information from him, her swift examination and dissection of every statement made, and now the amazingly serene expression on her face as she hummed to herself. He predicted her next question to himself and was pleased at his accuracy.

'Who was the victim?' She almost sang 'victim'. Not *my* victim, *the* victim. Smart lady, thought Number Four, smart lady indeed.

'There was no corpse,' said Arthur.

Her eyebrows arched. 'No corpse? Was there a trail of blood leading to the kitchen door?'

'No.'

'Doctor?'

'Yes?'

'No bruises on me other than the three scratches on my left cheek?'

'None.'

'Have any of Laura Denning's friends been reported missing?'

'No,' said Arthur.

'Anybody reported missing from Harborford?'

Number Four smiled as Arthur replied again, 'No one.'

'Do I keep livestock at the cottage, such as poultry?'

'Good heavens, *no*,' said Arthur. Arthur, she decided, does not favour poultry.

'Any pets?'

'No.'

'I trust the immediate neighbourhood has been fine-combed for a body.'

'The police are still looking.'

'The cottage is on a cliff?'

'Yes,' said Arthur.

'Well, it could have been flung over the cliff and washed out to sea.'

'There's a stretch of rocks at the bottom of the cliff. Even at high tide the water never covers them.'

'But there I sat in a cataleptic state at the table, in a blood-drenched kitchen holding a blood-stained knife, and unable to remember any of it.'

'Would you like a cup of tea, dear?' inquired Nurse Murdock professionally.

'Only if you can read the leaves,' replied the patient amiably. 'I would like a cigarette.'

'You don't smoke!' exclaimed Arthur.

Score one for me, she thought smugly, but I *do* smoke because I'm *dying* for a cigarette.

'You gave them up six months ago at my advice,' added Doctor Flint gently. 'Your bronchitis.'

'Oh,' she said. 'Well *toujours gaie* and whatthahell. I'd like a cigarette.' She held out her right hand and Arthur dug a cigarette from his pack, placed it in her hand and lit it for her. I got away with that one, she thought to herself. I didn't look for the cigarette. I waited until he placed it in my hand. I even fumbled putting it in my mouth. I hope I have a good reason for not wanting them to know I can see. I need time to think, that's why. Number Four *must* be a policeman.

'Doctor?'

'Yes, Laura?'

'Supposing this veil never lifts?'

'It will, I can assure you, it will.'

'Aren't there cases of amnesiacs who have never fully recovered, if at all?'

'Amnesia is a self-imposed condition brought on by stress . . .'

'Doctor,' she said with over-emphasised patience, 'a simple yes or no will do. Supposing I'm trapped in this void indefinitely, what then?'

'I have every reason to believe you will recover your memory.'

'Fifteen minutes ago you said my eyes would focus in a few seconds. I'm waiting, Doctor.'

'You're under a terrible strain.'

'This cigarette is stale.' She held it out and the nurse took it and stubbed it out in the ashtray. 'Is this a police hospital?'

'Goodness no, dear, I told you,' said Nurse Murdock, 'this is a private sanatorium.'

'Which private sanatorium?'

'Mine, Laura.' The doctor's voice now had an edge to it. 'You help support it.'

'I do? Arthur, make sure we get a rate.' The Doctor laughed politely and she resisted an urge to reach out and pinch his cherubic cheek. 'Number Four?'

'I feel rather absurd calling you Number Four. How are you listed with Scotland Yard?'

'Detective-Inspector Clive Fuller.'

She thought for a moment and then said, 'I think I know that name.'

'I published a thriller of his under a pseudonym,' said Arthur.

'Oh, Arthur, how lovely, you're a publisher. You must be terribly rich.'

'Not bad, my dear, not bad.'

'Do you publish me, too?'

'No,' he said glumly. 'You won't permit it.'

'Have we quarrelled over that?'

His face reddened. 'It's been discussed from time to time.'

'Mr Fuller?' He removed the pipe from his mouth and crossed to the left side of the bed. 'Have we met before?'

'No, Mrs Denning, we haven't.'

'Do you think I'm a murderess?'

He clamped the pipe back between his teeth.

'Well, do you? I don't suppose there's the mark of Cain on my forehead, but they do say murderers have certain specific characteristics.'

'Mrs Denning, you of all people should appreciate my position.'

'Chew on this for a change, Detective-Inspector. If I murdered someone, then disposed of the body . . . would I then return to my home, pick up the murder weapon, seat myself at a kitchen table and then will myself into a state of catalepsy? Hardly. I'd have cleaned up the place and myself and been prepared for the arrival of my husband come to spend the weekend . . .' and she stopped herself. 'But this all took place on a Monday, you say. Arthur would hardly have arrived for the weekend. Arthur is a publisher and on Monday should be in his office, because Monday is a very busy day in any successful profession. Arthur? What were you doing at Royalties on a Monday?'

'You sent for me.'

'Well, go on.'

'You phoned me late Sunday night and pleaded with me . . .'

*'Pleaded?'*

He sank into a chair and then leaned forward with his hands palms downward on his knees. 'We've been estranged for months.'

Her mouth formed the word 'Oh' but no sound emerged. She stroked her left cheek and could feel the traces of the scratches. 'Doctor, these must have been rather deep.'

'Yes.'

'They won't leave scars, will they?'

'No, no . . . they most certainly won't!'

'Arthur, this is terribly embarrassing for both of us.'

'The facts are known to everyone in this room.'

'Oh yes, of course, they would be under the circumstances. Number Four . . . oh . . . sorry . . . I mean Mr Fuller . . . could I speak to you alone please?'

Nurse Murdock was the last to leave the room, and gently shut the door behind her. She watched Arthur Denning cross the white corridor to a waiting room, and felt compassionately sorry for the man. Doctor Flint stood staring at the floor with his hands on his hips, shaking his head slowly from side to side.

'What's wrong, Doctor.'

'The woman in that bed is not the Laura Denning I knew.'

Nurse Murdock tensed. 'What do you mean?'

He directed his attention to the Nurse. 'I wish I knew what I meant. That's what's bothering me. I've treated amnesia cases before, but nothing like this. They usually panic. They cry. More often they're frightened and behave like children. But Laura Denning . . .'

Nurse Murdock laid it on the line. 'You think it's an act.'

The Doctor exhaled before speaking. 'If it's an act, it's a bloody brilliant one. You see, Miss Murdock, the private Laura Denning is a bright, witty and of course extremely brilliant woman. But the public Laura Denning is shy, aloof and withdrawn.' He folded his arms, shaking his head. 'But that woman in there,' with a jerk of his head towards the patient's room, 'that's a new personality altogether. I feel as though I'm meeting her for the first time.'

'Mr Fuller,' began the patient as soon as she saw the door shut, 'am I under arrest?'

He didn't answer immediately, occupying himself with drawing a straightback chair closer to the bed, sitting and clamping his teeth back around the pipe stem.

'Well am I?' she persisted, avoiding his face by focusing on the door knob, privately pleased with the thought that if Stanislavsky were alive and present he'd applaud her interpretation of his Method.

'Laura Denning should know there's no proof of a crime without a corpse.' His beautifully resonant voice stirred a distant memory of a college professor for whom she had nursed a secret infatuation until she'd noticed his shirt collars were dirty.

'Are you completely sold on Arthur's story?'

She suppressed a wince as his teeth ground down on the hapless pipe stem.

'Well now . . .' he finally said.

She decided he needed help. 'What I'm getting at is, there wasn't anyone with Arthur when he found me in the kitchen, was there?'

'No, he was quite alone.'

'Was I moved from the table before or after Doctor Kettering . . . is that the name . . .?'

'. . . Yes. . . .'

'. . . arrived at the cottage?'

'Your husband had carried you to the sitting room and placed you on the couch.'

'Still clutching the knife?'

'Yes.'

We must be *very* estranged, she thought with bristling indignation. Any truly devoted spouse would have pried loose the weapon, wiped it clean of fingerprints, run the blade under the tap in the kitchen, restored the knife to its proper drawer, shoved his hands in his pockets and returned to the sitting room whistling under his breath, silently commending himself on his loyalty. But not *our* Arthur.

'Still clutching the knife,' she repeated, it sounding to Fuller more like an imprecation than a statement.

'It took an injection from Doctor Kettering to relax your muscles.'

'That's not unusual?'

'Not in cataleptics.' She made a mental note to do some research of her own into catalepsy.

'Mr Fuller, I couldn't be the victim of some elaborate hoax, could I?'

He crossed his legs as she heard the pipe stem grate again and wondered if he had false teeth. 'If so, I should think it would be the work of a maniac. If someone was looking to get rid of you, short of murder there's a simpler method.'

'Such as?'

'Divorce.'

She smiled and then spoke. 'You have to admit it's not illogical this entire situation could have been staged by Arthur.'

'The past three weeks I've spent a great deal of time questioning Mr Denning.' Mr Denning. Not 'your husband'. 'I've concluded he's incapable of so extravagant a plot.'

'What a bore!' She hastily added, 'Your conclusion, not Arthur.' She sank into thought.

*Maybe it's the moon over Cornwall . . .*

'What's that tune you keep humming?'

'Hmmm?'

'That tune . . . the one you keep humming when you're thinking. . . .'

'Oh . . . do you suppose it might be significant?'

He leaned forward in his chair and she wasn't sure if the new note was one of urgency or irritation. 'I must admit, Mrs Denning, I am grasping at straws. I've been confronted with some seemingly impossible puzzles before, but to use one of your American expressions, this one's a lulu!'

One of *your* American expressions.

'I *thought* my accent was different!' she said joyfully, 'that explains Easthampton.'

'I beg your pardon?'

She explained her earlier association of the name Arthur with Easthampton. Three times he counterpointed with 'Good . . . Good . . . that's promising . . . very promising.'

'Why?' she asked after his 'very promising'.

'It indicates only a certain portion of your memory is blocked.'

'You mean I might work my way up from Easthampton to the day of the murder?' She wished she could retract 'murder'.

'So far, that's my only hope.'

'That might take years.' She found the thought consoling.

'You're humming again.' He said it very gently, almost sounding like an ally.

'Damn it, Mr Fuller, do *you* recognise the tune?'

'No. I wish I did.'

'Have you asked Arthur if I compose music as a hobby?'

'There's been no reason to. You only started humming today.'

'I could cry.'

'Go right ahead.'

'No. It would only embarrass us both. Could I see your credentials, please?'

'I was wondering when you'd get around to that.' He showed her his credentials and when she was satisfied he asked in a bland voice, 'How long have you had your vision?'

'Damn!' She sat upright, pounding the bed with both her fists, then folded her arms and sunk back against the pillows. 'I'm sure you understand, Mr Fuller, I feel victimised! When I asked you if I looked like a murderer, it was because I don't feel like a murderer! And if I *am* Laura Denning, then Laura Denning couldn't kill!'

'Why not?' The pipe stem scraped again.

'I see. You're another one who believes there's a potential killer in all of us.'

'Not all. Most.' Now her eyes searched the room frantically. 'What are you looking for?'

'A hand mirror.'

'I believe I saw one on the dressing table.' He crossed to the table and found the mirror near three neatly stacked books. He picked up the hand mirror and one of the books and returned to her.

She studied her face. Then she turned to stare at the book he was holding up for her to see. It was the back of the dust jacket which featured a photograph of the same face she saw reflected in the hand mirror, lacking only the three scratches on her left cheek.

'All right,' she said, 'I'm Laura Denning.' She returned the hand mirror which he placed on top of the book on the night table. 'So Arthur is my husband and we're estranged. How long has that been going on?'

'Close to a year.'

'What explanation did he give you?'

'It seems you began drifting apart shortly after you acquired Royalties.'

'What was I doing in Harborford in the first place?'

'You'd spent your honeymoon there eight years ago.'

'And then, I suppose, it occasioned many sentimental journeys.'

'At least two or three times a year until you settled into Royalties.'

She threw up her hands in despair. 'This is unreal! It's so cold-blooded, so dispassionate, the way I feel when I'm researching a book!'

'Ah!' Their eyes met and both smiled.

'That was a step forward, wasn't it.' She felt the least he could do was pat her on the head and present her with a sweet, but then she worried she might have a tail to wag. 'So I'm remembering how it felt researching a book.' A coldness settled over her and she embraced herself.

He asked with genuine concern, 'Are you feeling ill? You've turned pale.'

'It's just hit me. Supposing I *have* killed someone?'

28

He settled back in the chair. 'You can afford the best lawyers.'

'That was equally cold and dispassionate.'

'I have to be in this job. You know that.'

She nodded as the warmth began to return and wondered aloud if he also smoked cigarettes. He didn't.

'All right. So I settle into Royalties and Arthur and I begin drifting apart. Professional reasons or mutual boredom?'

Fuller removed the pipe from his mouth. 'He suspects you have a lover.'


Chapter Three

The manner in which he imparted her suspected infidelity released the brief memory of a dreadful film she recalled seeing, highlighted momentarily by a Russian peasant woman bursting into a crowded salon to announce the birth of Peter Ilyitch Tschaikowsky. She drew her feet up and wrapped her hands around her knees. I, Laura Denning (and there's no denying my identity now unless in the past three weeks someone's come up with instant plastic surgery) should be a thoroughly contented woman. I am a successful writer, I am wealthy, I have a seemingly devoted husband, I own the cottage of my dreams and yet *'He suspects you have a lover.'*

Fuller shifted in his chair. 'You look very pleased with yourself.'

'It's nice to know the scholar isn't a stick-in-the-mud.'

'But that's the contradiction. You're supposed to be.'

She released her knees and turned on her side, propping her head up with her right hand. 'In Arthur's opinion?'

Fuller nodded, adding, 'Corroborated by acquaintances and business associates, and further substantiated by Doctor

29

Flint. You are shy, aloof and withdrawn. You have no close friends.'

'How awful!'

'You are totally dedicated to your work and hell to live with, especially when writing.'

'Then Arthur shouldn't give a damn if I've found a lover.' She repositioned herself and was upright again. 'And if I'm absolute hell to live with when I'm writing, then that explains the cottage. There I have the peace and solitude I require while he's in London. . . .'

'Yes?' She never dreamt she'd ever hear that word spoken with such eagerness.

'You know damned well what I'm thinking. If our Arthur is a normal man with a normal appetite he could very well have a mistress!'

'He doesn't.' She subsided. 'Or at least I haven't found any signs of one.' How, she wondered, does one *find* signs of a mistress? Are they expected to pop out of the ground once a year to cast a shadow, or is there some form of rabbit-test known only to Scotland Yard? She said as much to which he replied, 'I have thoroughly investigated your husband. Forgive me, but you're of a kind. He is shy, aloof and withdrawn . . . which is what brought you together . . . in Easthampton.' She felt air entering her mouth and realised her chin had dropped. 'He was in America on a business trip, your first book was successfully published and he was after it, friends arranged for you to meet at a weekend house party, he didn't get the book but he got you.'

'I'd like to think it was a fair exchange. I wonder if I was madly in love with him when he popped the question or too shy and aloof to say *no*.'

'You don't much fancy the Arthur Denning you've met today, do you?'

She buried her face in her hands and shook her head: 'No.' A fresh thought struck her and she released her face. 'Since emerging from my coma I haven't been exactly shy, aloof *or* withdrawn, have I?'

30

'Quite the contrary, which is why I tend to believe a lover isn't all that unlikely. People have been known to change over a period of time. For example, you're quite a different person in Harborford.'

I'll bet I am, she thought ruefully, my decor the envy of every housewife. Who but Laura Denning would be clever enough to decorate her kitchen with bloodstains. 'Tell me about me in Harborford.'

He produced a match from his pocket, ignited it with a thumbnail and applied the flame to the pipe bowl. It relieved her to know the pipe wasn't merely a prop. It also gave her time to study his face. The bone structure was good and the nose was just short of being a promontory. His skin looked smooth and unveined, but judging from the dark shadow that ran from ear to ear he'd need a shave in about three hours. His hair was light brown dappled with grey and she decided his were probably Scottish origins. The pipe bowl was a miniature Vesuvius and he placed the dead match in the ashtray.

'You're rather well-liked in Harborford.'

'That's a comfort.'

'They respect your work and are pleased that you've settled among them.'

'I hope they still feel that way after the late unpleasantness.'

He studied the pipe bowl for a moment and then told her, 'Harborford doesn't know what we found at the cottage other than Doctor Kettering and the police, and they can be trusted of course.'

'You're so sure.'

'Quite sure. You're a celebrity and there's been nothing in the newspapers, so there's been no leak.'

'I'm sure there's method to this madness.'

'It's method, hardly madness. If you're not the actual murderer, we'd like the killer to feel safe and over-confident.'

'And perhaps strike again?'

Fuller burst into laughter and even that matched the personality. It was sincere but controlled. When the laughter subsided, he took a thoughtful drag on the pipe and then said, 'The tradespeople especially like you and that's always a recommendation in a small village.'

'Maybe the air down there does something to me.'

'The Laura Denning I'm describing only began to emerge about a year after she purchased the cottage.'

She studied her fingernails and realised to her horror a manicure was long overdue. 'Presumably about the time I might have taken a lover?' A smoke ring missed her nose by a fraction of an inch and he apologised. She politely admired it and then pursued Harborford. 'Well who *is* he?' She hoped it was someone she liked.

'Haven't a clue.'

'Oh for crying out loud! Then how dare Arthur!'

'Apparently you haven't shared your husband's bed in more than a year. The total estrangement came about shortly after Christmas ... over six months ago ... when you settled into Royalties permanently. You haven't seen your husband since then. Is it no wonder he suspects a lover?'

Laura leaned forward. 'Has it ever occurred to you, Mr Fuller, that I no longer desired my husband's favours, to put it delicately? That eventually does happen to one or the other partner in a bloodless marriage. Besides which, I don't *feel* as though I have a lover.'

'You have amnesia.'

'Oh stuff the bloody amnesia!' She realised she was bouncing and stopped. 'Amnesia or no amnesia, shouldn't my subconscious be prodding me into missing the touch of *that* hand, a desire to hear *that* voice, all that cornball junk you read in women's magazines?'

'I don't read women's magazines.'

'Well *I* do.' She smiled shyly. 'I do, you know. It gives me confidence when I think my writing powers are flagging. It makes me realise I'm better than I think I am.'

'You don't remember Arthur.'

'You've *met* Arthur!' She spoke too hastily and felt ashamed. 'Sorry. That was cruel.'

'It was honest.'

'Why did I phone Arthur from the cottage that Sunday night? As I recall, he says I *pleaded* with him . . . for what? Certainly not a reconciliation.'

'That was the impression you gave him.'

'What did I actually say?' She was pounding the bed again and he stayed her hand with a gesture of his own. She folded her arms and sank back against the pillows, hoping her throbbing temples wouldn't burst.

'He doesn't remember your actual words, but however you put it, it was enough for him to rush down the next morning. You're humming again.'

'I know, I know.' She stared at the ceiling for a moment and made a mental note to remind Doctor Flint the room needed redecorating. 'Arthur said I sounded frantic on the phone. For "frantic", couldn't we read "frightened"?'

'We could and I've taken that into consideration.'

'Thank you. Let's get back to my lover. I assume Arthur suspects someone in Harborford.'

'There are several prospects.'

She felt like a spinster consulting a marriage broker.

'Such as?'

He reached into his inside jacket pocket and produced a notebook. He rifled the pages until he found the one he needed. He stared at the page for a moment, then murmured 'Oh' and in his other inside jacket pocket found a pair of spectacles. Spectacles adjusted, he consulted the page again.

'Sean Coleridge.' He looked at her face. It was a blank. 'The name means nothing to you?'

'I'm thinking of "The Ancient Mariner" but that's another Coleridge.'

'Not bad though. He owns a fishing boat. You've made several trips with him and he's been a fairly frequent visitor

33

to the cottage.'

'Is he gorgeous?'

Fuller exploded into a coughing fit. He struggled for a handkerchief in his back pocket, covered his mouth, embarrassedly uncovered his mouth and removed his pipe, covered his mouth again and briefly resembled an antique steam engine struggling uphill. When he regained his composure he wiped his eyes and gave Laura a description of Sean Coleridge.

The mariner appeared to be in his late thirties, medium height with a lean and muscular body. A one-time merchant seaman, he had invested his life savings in his boat *Atlantis*, and catered frequently to private fishing parties. According to Fuller, Coleridge seemed well-educated, had a wry sense of humour and rugged good looks. Fuller looked up from his notebook and asked Laura, 'Why the cynical smile?'

'What excuse do you give these people when you question them? And what about my sudden absence from Harborford, how do you explain that?'

'You were attacked by a mysterious prowler whose motive might have been robbery and your husband took you back to London to recover. I didn't think it was too bad on the spur of the moment.'

'And everyone's bought that?' Fuller nodded. 'I've told no one Arthur and I are separated?'

'If you have, I didn't get an inkling in Harborford. Not even a raised eyebrow.'

'Strange.'

'Why?'

Laura leaned forward. 'Wouldn't it have seemed more likely after this mythical invasion I'd have s.o.s.'d my hypothetical lover?'

'It would,' agreed Fuller, 'but strangely enough, not one of your husband's candidates called the bluff.'

'Some lover,' said Laura after a snort. Then she rationalised, 'Unless of course my hero has something to hide.'

'Precisely.'

She wondered if Fuller was married and was then annoyed with herself for the conjecture. 'How did you explain yourself to Harborford?'

'You're Laura Denning. Arthur has influential connections with Scotland Yard. Harborford is too small for a police force of any consequence, just two local constables.'

'Day shift and night shift?'

'Just about.' He indicated his notebook. 'Shall I continue?' Laura nodded. 'Frank Welbeck.'

'The sculptor?'

Fuller lowered the notebook and folded his arms. 'You don't recall his estate is less than a mile from your cottage?'

Laura frowned. 'I suppose I might have read that in some newspaper article. Hasn't he become some sort of recluse? Bought an old castle or some such, then holed up there with a sister or whatever ... oh for God's sake help me!'

He wondered if he was being perverse in finding her frustration so appealing. There was an undefinable arrogance when she pouted and perhaps arrogance was the wrong word, it was more a mixture of strength and defiance. He respected strength but abhorred defiance in women. He disliked masculine women and to him masculine and defiance were synonymous. He also disliked feminine aggressiveness. Yet in Laura Denning the ingredients seemed to add up to an attractive personality and he realised she was staring at him with a quizzical expression. He popped the pipe back into his mouth and glanced swiftly at the notebook.

'Welbeck's immersed in the biggest project of his career.' He looked up. 'Twelve life-size sculptures of infamous women in history.'

'Heavens,' she gasped.

'I've seen the five he's completed.' He listed Catherine de Medici, Lucrezia Borgia, Cleopatra, Sappho and Marie Antoinette. On another occasion, Laura would have spiritedly debated 'infamous' as descriptive of at least two

35

of the subjects but pigeon-holed it for a more appropriate occasion should it ever present itself. 'His work-in-progress is Charlotte Corday. You've been modelling for Charlotte.'

'Oh, charming; Laura Denning found with a blood-stained knife in her hand modelling for Marat's assassin. It's all *too* penny-dreadful.'

'Just an unfortunate coincidence. They happen.'

'I remember this much about Welbeck. He's a dedicated artist and a dedicated brother. That sister . . .'

'. . . Emaline,' he interjected.

'. . . Perfect . . . guards him with what reads to me like an unnatural possessiveness!'

'She adores you.'

'I can't win.'

'You frequently do.' Her head shot up. 'At bridge. You've been playing bridge at the Welbecks at least twice a week. He's a very shy, very lonely man. He relates to very few people. You're one of the chosen few.'

'I thought it was opposites that attracted. Obviously I'm an isolated case. I marry shy Arthur, I'm attracted to shy Welbeck, and what about Coleridge, does he bury his nose in fishing tackle?'

'Somewhat!'

'Oh, good!' she snapped. 'Let's not flaw the lady's pattern. What other shrinking violets do you have in store for me?'

'Doctor Kettering.'

At last, she said to herself, now I know how a tyre feels when the air's been let out of it. Aloud she inquired, 'And there's no *Mrs* Kettering?'

'He's a widower.' She thought this deserved a violin accompaniment, but didn't mention it.

'Am I supposed to have an unbridled passion for the good doctor?'

'I won't have the vaguest idea how you feel about any of them until you're able to tell me.'

'Deduction is your business! You've met me and you've

met them!' She didn't seem aware she was waving her hands like a woman trying to dry the fresh polish on her nails. 'Every detective I ever met when researching my books was an armchair psychiatrist, surely you've come to *some* conclusion about me and these men?'

'Yes. Arthur is a jealous husband.'

Her hands dropped palms upward and she stared at them. The heart line in her right palm was broken in two places and her lifeline almost met her wrist, and that gave her small comfort. Arthur. I have to get to know Arthur. I have to meet these people in Harborford. I have to see Harborford. And Royalties. The kitchen. She told all this to Fuller.

'We'll see,' he said quietly.

Instinct warned her not to pursue the matter. Instead she asked, 'How long has Dr Kettering been a widower?'

'Ohhhh,' he stared at the ceiling as though expecting to find the answer printed there, 'some two years or so.'

'No children?'

'None.' He'd abandoned the ceiling for his notebook. 'They'd only been married about a year when the tragedy occurred.'

Bright sunlight was streaming through the window and she was covered with a heavy quilt, yet she felt cold. 'What tragedy?' Fuller had lit another match and was sucking on the pipestem. When the bowl was lit and the match discarded, he spoke.

'It was a Sunday fishing party on Coleridge's boat. Mid-morning, the boat was hit by a sudden squall. Before the party could make it below decks, a huge wave hit the boat. Mrs Kettering was swept overboard.'

Laura felt her mouth go dry but managed to whisper, 'How awful.'

'Yes,' agreed Fuller, 'even now Kettering speaks of it with difficulty. It was a small party. In addition to the crew there was Coleridge of course, the Ketterings, the Welbecks . . .'

'And me,' she said sharply.

'And you. You were holding Viola Kettering's hand when the wave struck.'

## Chapter Four

Clive Fuller hated hospitals, long interrogations and tears. Hating hospitals was a throwback to his early teens and a six-month siege of tuberculosis. Long interrogations usually led to a short temper, his own, but the day before Laura Denning emerged from her coma, he had prepared himself for what he foresaw as a long verbal siege. However, he was unprepared for her amnesia. If she doesn't stop crying soon, he thought privately, I may have to send for a pair of aqua-lungs. What he didn't know was that Laura Denning was a past master at sustaining tears, especially when she needed time to think. Arthur could have told him that, but Arthur was still exiled to the waiting room, sitting in an easy chair, puffing a cigar, reading *The New Statesman* and sipping a cup of lukewarm tea thoughtfully provided by Nurse Murdock.

Besides which, and the thought provided Fuller with an inexplicable discomfort for reasons he couldn't fathom then, he was enjoying telling Laura Denning about Laura Denning. She was beginning to know herself again, but he was getting to know her better. He had the advantage of perspective, she had to accept what she was told as gospel until she could prove otherwise, if there was otherwise to be proven.

Her insistent desire to return as soon as possible to Harborford pleased him and increased his growing admiration for the spunky woman. He had accepted the case by special request and influence of Arthur Denning, it having forced the postponement of a long-awaited fishing trip in Scotland. But Arthur Denning was his publisher, his book had lost money, and he considered accepting the case a form of refund. The week he spent in Harborford investigating and interrogating had been a difficult one, far more difficult than he had admitted to Laura. He couldn't be sure everyone bought his fabrication for Laura's sudden absence from the village. If there had been an anonymous attack, he realised every person he spoke to saw themselves as a suspect. But two people had answered his questions openly and seemingly without guile, as though any guilts they might have haboured were those of childhood indiscretions long since dismissed.

Of graver concern to Fuller was not whó was attacked or who committed the crime, but why. Motive usually revealed itself unconsciously, it was something he relied on in all interrogations after his years of experience, but no such thing emerged in Harborford. There were expressions of petty dislikes and disapprovals, but nothing to indicate the possibility of murder unless his perception was failing him, and he was too much of an egotist to accept that.

He realised Laura was babbling through her tears. She was convinced she was a Jonah, a jinx and ill-starred and must have suffered brain damage as a child, the way some adult heart cases are the result of childhood rheumatic fever. Fuller did his best to reassure her but she was having none of it.

'You're implying I might have shoved that woman overboard!' Fuller assured her he wasn't and Laura accepted the tissue he offered her and unsuccessfully attempted to staunch the tears.

*That woman.* She repeated the words to herself. What was her name again? Viola? I must have liked her. We were probably friends, why else partake of her company even if that particular Sunday promised the safety of group activity. I was holding her hand. Tightly? Not tightly enough. Slowly, she lowered the hand holding the damp tissue and stared ahead, now even deeper in thought.

Why was *I* holding her hand? Why not one of the men, specifically her husband. Perhaps we were separated from the men when the storm broke, but a storm at sea can certainly be seen coming. Sean Coleridge as captain of the boat should have given us sufficient warning to get below. Certainly Dr Kettering should have had enough concern for his wife to find her and guide her to safety.

'Did Kettering tell you I was holding his wife's hand?'

'No,' replied Fuller, grateful the flood had abated and her mind was working again, 'Emaline Welbeck. She wasn't implying any sinister motive, I assure you. What happened was, the wave caused the boat to lurch, Viola Kettering stumbled against the rail, you grabbed for her hand, caught it, but Viola panicked, lost your grip and went overboard. When the men got you and Emaline below, you had hysterics.'

'What about Emaline?' she asked abruptly.

'What do you mean?'

'What was *her* reaction to the tragedy?'

His face reddened. 'It never occured to me to ask her.'

*Maybe it's the moon over* ... 'Damn it!' she snapped in mid-hum, 'I'm beginning to hate that tune. I wonder if Arthur knows it. Maybe it's ...' punctuating the moment with a shrug, '... *our* song.'

'He had no comment for it earlier, but we can ask him.'

'Yes, we must do that. Coleridge, Kettering and the Welbecks,' she mused. 'Is that it?'

'They're only Arthur's contribution. There are a few others.' He referred to the notebook again. 'There's Auriol Kendall and her niece, Fiona Cooper. Miss Kendall paints water colours, most of which she sells to birthday greetings manufacturers.' Laura envisaged a sparrow-like, near-sighted lady in a paint-stained smock, probably in her late sixties and a jam preserver in her spare time. Fuller described a tall, handsome woman in her mid-fifties, favouring tweeds and 'sensible' shoes, a chain-smoker, partial to boiled sweets. 'She consumed half a bottle the afternoon I spent with her.'

'What about Fiona?'

'I didn't meet the niece.'

Laura's head shot forward. 'Why not?'

'She was away on a field trip. Lepidopterist.'

'Did she leave before or *after* my unfortunate Monday.'

'Early that morning. I'm beginning to loathe that song.'

She stopped humming and murmured 'Sorry. I suppose Fiona's a spinster.'

'Yes. I saw a photo. There's one on the piano in their cottage which adjoins the Welbeck estate. It's draped with a Spanish shawl.'

'The cottage?'

'The piano.'

Spanish-shawl-draped piano, thought Laura. The ladies have no taste. 'What did the photo tell you about Fiona?'

'Rather attractive. Blond, slim, good features and about as tall as Miss Kendall. They're standing alongside each other in the photo.' He was attacking the ashtray with the pipebowl and Laura began to suspect she disliked woodpeckers. 'She looks a bit like you do, as a matter of fact. I thought it was a photo of you at first.'

'Are you sure it *wasn't*?'

'Yes. You took the picture.'

'That was right neighbourly of me.'

'You met the Welbecks through them. Fiona was the model for Welbeck's statue of Sappho.'

'Which one did Viola pose for?' The question emerged so rapidly, she even startled herself.

'Catherine de Medici,' was his equally rapid reply.

'Which did Emaline model?'

'Lucrezia Borgia.'

'That leaves Cleopatra and Marie Antoinette.'

'Professional models imported from London. They were before you bought Royalties.'

'How did I meet the aunt and niece?'

'It seems one morning Fiona was chasing a butterfly across your grounds, tripped on her net and landed in your begonias. You offered her a cup of tea and the friendship began, or so Miss Kendall told me.'

'I'll bet there's more to that aunt and niece than met your eye. Nobody's infallible, Mr Fuller.'

He agreed with that, but wished she hadn't said it so pointedly. 'There's more to everyone in Harborford than meets the eye, but I didn't have all that much time to stick around and study them.'

'You'll have to go back then.'

'From the looks of it now, yes. Doctor Flint warned me before you became conscious there might be loss of memory. Of course I hoped against it, that you'd be able to tell me exactly what happened. But you can't and I can see it's going to take time.'

'I'm going there too,' she stated flatly. Their eyes met and the challenge in hers was stronger than a tax evader under investigation. 'I know you can't prove murder because you haven't produced a victim. Oh you might try holding me as a material witness or some protective custody nonsense, but you know as well as I do that you *need* me back in Harborford. My return is going to make somebody nervous and nervous people make mistakes and other people's mistakes can often prove profitable.'

'It can be dangerous.'

She waved her hand airily. 'You'll be there to protect me.'

'It can't be my decision. There are people I answer to.'

Laura leaned forward conspiratorially. 'You'll swing it. My money's on you.'

In Fuller's private opinion, Charlotte Corday was a mistake. Laura should have posed for Cleopatra.

Five minutes later, Laura was alone, frightened, worried and hungry. She had reclaimed the hand mirror from the night table and was giving her reflection an intensive

42

examination. It felt strange not to recognise herself. It was as though she actually had undergone plastic surgery and was having a difficult time making up her mind if she liked her new face. Some day, she told herself ruefully, you'll know yourself again and then you might wish you'd never recovered from this amnesia. Amnesia. That's something that happens to other people, like plane crashes. On the other hand, and this new thought began to delight her, at some future date (years perhaps? Good God, pray not) at dinner or a cocktail party, she could see herself astonishing some guest with, 'A few months ago when I was suffering from amnesia . . .' She could hardly wait. She felt here was a form of Oneupmanship even Stephen Potter would have admired.

She placed the hand mirror back on the night table and settled back against the pillows with her hands folded. Fuller had fed her so much and it all needed to be digested. Sean Coleridge. The Welbecks. Auriol Kendall and Fiona Cooper. The Ketterings. Dr *Who* Kettering? What first name? *Maybe it's the moon over Cornwall. . . .* Bloody tune. Arthur. I have to talk to Arthur. What does an amnesiac say to an estranged husband? 'Listen, honey, since I don't remember a thing, let's take it from the top and . . .' Oh God. *Do I have any other family?* Yes, a consultation with Arthur is unavoidable. I have to know as much about me as I can before I tackle Harborford. I don't know why it's all that necessary, but somehow I feel it is. I know why! Because I'm Laura Denning and Laura Denning is a perfectionist! Her books are carefully researched and brilliantly constructed and her deductions are astonishingly original and logical. I must have read *all* of Laura Denning. Of course you did you damned fool, she reminded herself almost with embarrassment, you *are* Laura Denning. She reached out and picked up the Denning book from the night table.

*Beyond a Black Veil.*

She turned to the page listing the author's previous

works and was more than proud of herself. Seven books and still in her early thirties! What an achievement! I guess my only failure between covers was Arthur.

Shy, aloof, diffident.

*But that's not me at all! Not now it isn't!*

I'll buy it from childhood through my first five years of marriage. But something happened in Harborford. Something happened to alter my personality from the time I acquired the cottage and saw less of Arthur.

Saw less of Arthur.

She sat up. *Arthur.* Opposites usually attract, but in her and Arthur's case it didn't. The Harborford men Fuller described were apparently cut from the same cloth. But she had told Fuller he wasn't infallible, and there's more to someone in Harborford than met Fuller's eye. Something, someone in that village was responsible for bringing her out of herself, caused her to go cold on Arthur.

You're humming again, you idiot, stop it.

I wonder who cleaned up the kitchen after I was taken to London. Fuller? The two constables? Dr Kettering? All four? Did Fuller bring other detectives with him when he came to the village? Damn! There's so much to know, so much to find out. *Who was the victim?*

She placed the book to one side. She needed her fingers to press against her temples.

Think. *Think!* she willed herself. Try to remember what happened that morning. You phoned Arthur Sunday night and . . . Her hands dropped. Why couldn't the murder have happened *Sunday night?* Just because Arthur found me shortly after two p.m. the following day, does it necessarily follow the blood was spilled on Monday? It could have been Sunday night and then I phoned Arthur. . . .

Arthur, she wondered, are you possibly withholding vital information? Are you lying about the conversation that took place between us if a conversation *did* take place? There's direct-dialling now in England (I remember *that*!) but I suppose (and her shoulders sagged) that can still be

44

traced, my call to Arthur. I probably did call Arthur, but what did I actually say? Yes, I must positively talk to Arthur.

She hungered for more than food. She wanted a notebook and pencil. She wanted to get to work on 'the mysterious affair at Royalties'. Heavens, she thought with delight, *this* could be my next book!

She fell back against the pillows. I'm a very prolific writer. Doesn't it stand to reason I've been *working* on a book? Unless I recently completed one and sent it to my publisher, and if so, I'm sure he adores it. But if there's a work in progress . . .

Her thoughts were interrupted by Nurse Murdock entering briskly, balancing a tray of food with her left hand.

'Hungry, I hope!' she exclaimed cheerfully as she crossed to the bed and laid the tray across Laura's lap and plumped up the pillows. Laura lifted the metal cover from the largest plate and studied a slice of rare roast beef, a portion of limp leaf spinach that was more brown then green, and some mashed potatoes with a puddle of gravy in the centre.

'Is Mr Denning still here?'

'Yes, dear,' said Nurse Murdock surveying tray and patient like a priest about to bless a union. 'He's in the Doctor's office with Mr Fuller.'

'Could you tell him I'd like to see him when he's free?'

'Doctor says you've had enough excitement for one day.'

Knife and fork were poised in mid-air. 'What's so exciting about Arthur?'

Nurse Murdock blushed, frowned and then said solemnly, 'You've had no solid food in over three weeks. Please try to eat your dinner.'

Laura attacked the meat savagely, and after a few moments inquired without looking up, 'Nurse Murdock, could you ring for a buzz saw?'

Dr Flint's office overlooked a private park belonging to

45

the sanatorium, and from the window where Clive Fuller stood looking out he saw a magnificent view of the city. He also saw reflected in the window the tired man who was himself, Doctor Flint leaning over his desk to accept a light from Arthur Denning for a cigar also contributed by the publisher, and Denning's hand holding the lighter trembling slightly. Fuller had just finished telling them his plan to take Laura back to Harborford. When the Doctor's cigar was lit, Denning lit his own and then turned in the leather chair he occupied to speak to Fuller.

'I feel very uneasy about this, Clive, very uneasy indeed. If there's some other murderer at large,' (the words *some other murderer* now indelible in Fuller's mind) 'then Laura's not safe.' He drew on the cigar, rolled the smoke around his mouth, exhaled and said fiercely, 'I'm thoroughly against it.' He swerved towards the Doctor. 'You agree with me, don't you?' Dr Flint looked as noncommittal as a housewife on a television commercial making up her mind between the advertised product and Brand X.

Fuller broke the silence. 'Mrs Denning insists on returning there.'

Arthur leapt from the chair and slammed his fist on the desk. 'She's a damned fool!'

'She's a very brave woman,' snapped Fuller, wishing he hadn't sounded like Colonel Blimp. 'Amnesia or no amnesia, she still hasn't forgotten how to exercise her brain and she isn't buying a third of what she's been told.'

'I suppose if this is made official, I can't fight it,' retreated Arthur.

'There's every possibility she's been the victim of a cruel plot.'

'You didn't think that yesterday!'

'I didn't know Mrs Denning then.'

'Ah. I see.' Ah. You don't, thought Fuller, you can't see past the tip of your cigar. You'd like the entire matter hushed-up. Bad publicity. Bad show. Bad for the image, not

46

just Laura's, your publishing house's as well. But how long does something like this stay hushed-up? Harborford is suspicious now and Harborford gossips. Gossip proliferates, spreads, grows and can destroy. I don't like you, Arthur Denning, and that's probably the most important thing your wife and I have in common at the moment.'

Denning leaned across the desk facing Doctor Flint. 'Can Laura's mind take another shock?' Doctor Flint was pulling at an ear lobe, wondering if he'd have to miss another episode of *Coronation Street*. The question was logical yet ridiculous. How to reply to it without first subjecting Laura to a series of intensive tests? He finally said as much but Arthur didn't seem satisfied.

Arthur Denning didn't know it, but for the past few minutes he was playing hopscotch in Clive Fuller's mind. He hopped from box to box on an unsteady leg. Each box had a label. Estrangement. Fear. Cowardice. Lies.

'It would look better if you came with us,' Fuller said to Denning. Denning straightened and their eyes met.

'Yes, yes I suppose it would. I ... I'll discuss it with Laura.' He mustered an awkward smile. 'The estrangement, you know. I'm not very good at play acting.'

There, thought Fuller, we disagree again.


It was while almost gagging on a spoonful of something that Nurse Murdock unashamedly insisted to the patient was a strawbery mousse and not an enlarged blood clot, that a fresh idea surfaced in Laura's mind. *Surely, surely this must have occured to Fuller*. The thought made her flush with excitement and Nurse Murdock mistakenly attributed the colour in Laura's cheeks to an overheated room and moved to open the window.

'Don't!' commanded Laura, who thought the room was an icebox, and then demanded her bag. While Nurse Murdock removed the tray and herself, Laura applied lipstick, powder and mascara, and then settled back to wait for Arthur.

47

It *must* have occurred to Fuller.

Arthur arrived, pecked her cheek like a dying housefly making one last swipe at a block of cheddar, and then settled into a straightbacked chair with his legs crossed. She endured the ensuing solicitations with remarkable patience, and then subjected him to a detailed cross-examination. She learned she had been orphaned as a child, her parents perishing in an automobile crash after a night of Bingo at the local church in the town of her birth in upstate New York. She lived with her mother's parents until matriculating at Smith College and so on *ad infinitum*. He repeated the details of their meeting and courtship as told to her earlier by Fuller. He launched into her success as a writer which did not interest her so she rudely cut him short. Then with an air of coquetry she had always imagined reserved for fat women angling for a compliment on their thin ankles, she asked, 'What did you *ever* see in quiet, shy, introverted little me?'

'Oh but you weren't like that at all,' he said, 'you were gay and vivacious, the life of the party the night we met!'

'So what happened to me?' From the look on Arthur's face, she felt she knew how one of Fiona Cooper's butterflies felt when it was pinned. He smiled weakly but said nothing. The look on his face corroborated everything Laura suspected. To make the marriage succeed, she must have done all the work. A quiet wife for a quiet man. My God, she thought, I must have loved him very deeply. I probably thought at the time I'd change *him*. She thought of reaching over and patting his hand, but didn't, and assuaged her tiny guilt by reassuring herself that had she done so, she might have fallen out of bed.

Arthur found his voice and babbled inanely about themselves and their dreams and their hopes and Laura stifled a yawn. As far as she was concerned he was rambling on about total strangers. It was time to interrupt him. She repeated the suspicion he imparted to Fuller of her having a lover in Harborford. He explained himself matter-of-factly.

48

He might have been discussing yesterday's cricket scores. There was logic to his reasoning and she found no cause to dispute it. He told her she was a healthy, attractive woman with a normal appetite for love and (he mumbled the word) sex, and if she wasn't servicing (his word) him, it stood to reason there was another recipient of her favours (also his word). She found herself feeling sorry for Arthur and aloud hoped he had a mistress.

He said diffidently, 'Well you know how it is, my dear.'

She wanted to say, 'No, but I really hope you do,' but instead said, 'I hope you're making the most of it,' which wasn't any better.

He leaned forward and said with conviction, 'I still love you, Laura.'

'I think what's important now, Arthur, is that we help Mr Fuller get to the bottom of this mess I'm in,' which led to an intense discussion of the proposed return to Harborford. It continued for about five minutes. Voices rose and fell like waves breaking against a beach, but the conclusion was inevitable.

'Then I shall be coming too,' said Arthur. Her eyes widened and he explained: 'Fuller thinks it would look better.'

Laura gave it some thought and agreed, 'You can use the guest room of course. We have one, haven't we?'

'There are four bedrooms,' said Arthur. She sagged against the pillows with her eyes closed. 'You must be very tired.' Her eyes opened slowly.

'Arthur, what did I really say to you the night I phoned.'

He shifted in his chair. 'I don't remember your exact words, of course.'

'You said I had pleaded with you.'

'You were . . . well . . . a bit frantic.'

'Frightened?'

'It sounded that way, yes. I thought at first you were drunk, but you don't drink that much.'

'What did I *say*?'

'Well, in so many words you implied there was trouble with someone. I thought perhaps you wanted a reconciliation. Well . . . you know . . . I thought the trouble was with him.'

'Who?'

'Whomever you're involved with!'

'And I was convincing enough for you to come the next morning?'

'I couldn't very well come that night. It was after midnight.' Laura catalogued that. 'There were no trains. I had put the car in for servicing and couldn't get it till the next morning. I must say, I drove like a demon!'

Laura persisted. 'I didn't mention any names? I didn't give a clue as to what had me frightened?'

'No. You said it was impossible to tell me on the phone, I remember that much quite clearly.'

Then at the time, thought Laura, I couldn't have thought there was any immediate danger. But whatever it was that frightened me, I turned to Arthur, not to any of my three, stalwart, local gentlemen. Nor to either of Harborford's two constables. 'You know *all* my friends in Harborford, don't you, Arthur?'

'Certainly.'

She sighed. 'Thank you, Arthur. You've been very helpful. You've eased my mind a great deal.' He hadn't, but she thought it a good idea to seem kindly disposed to Arthur, especially if he was to be underfoot at the cottage.

There was a knock at the door and Fuller stuck his head in. 'Just wanted to tell you I'll be by again in the morning.'

Laura sat bolt upright. 'You're just the man I want to see! Please come in! Arthur you've been a dear and you'll drop in again soon, won't you?'

'Why, I'll be by tomorrow!'

'Of course! Tomorrow!' His lips sideswiped her cheek again and with a curt goodnight to Fuller, he left. She asked Fuller to sit down. He selected a spot on the edge of the bed and the implied intimacy pleased her. 'Now then,

Mr Fuller, about the victim.'

'Yes?' His face brightened.

'Mr Fuller, surely it has occured to you there's another possible explanation as to why no body's been found?'

The pipe stem was headed for his mouth. 'Go on.'

'Isn't it possible *our* blood-stained victim left the cottage *alive*?'


Chapter Five

The village of Harborford consisted of little more than the High Street, which contained a butcher, a chemist, a greengrocer, a church, a town hall, a combination bakery and post office, and a brave little art gallery where tourists could also purchase souvenirs. The High Street extended to the wooden pier where there was a small marina for pleasure craft and the few commercial fishermen who plied its surrounding waters. One side of the peninsula was chalk cliffs and on these cliffs sat the homes of the local celebrities including the Welbeck estate, Auriol Kendall's cottage and Laura's.

During the early thirties, Harborford was something of an artist's colony. When the war came, travel restrictions sent the village into its artistic decline and only in the past decade occurred the small attempt to reclaim its once-colourful heritage. Its population according to the last census was a little over three hundred people. At the height of the summer season, the local inn, the Grace and Favour, carried its capacity of thirty guests. These were mostly the fishing parties who sustained Sean Coleridge's seasonal income.

The season was now under way, and Doctor Edmund Kettering could also count on its adding some shillings to his small, albeit comfortable yearly earnings. Fishing hooks

51

caught in hands or legs, prescriptions for seasick pills, ptomaine poisoning and the occasional case of sunstroke. On the morning of the day Laura Denning emerged from her coma, Edmund Kettering was attempting to surface from the depths of a depression.

It was a daily depression dating from the afternoon Arthur Denning had summoned him to the cottage where he'd found Laura on the couch in her cataleptic state clutching the blood-stained carving knife. When he saw the condition of the kitchen, he realised even doctors weren't immune to nausea. Then, injecting Laura to relax her muscles, the urgent summons to Doctor Flint, the arrival of Flint with Fuller, the minute examination of the premises, the spiriting of Laura back to London after midnight under a cloak of secrecy, the detailed interrogation by Fuller and then, finally, around two in the morning, with the aid of the constables, scrubbing down the kitchen until there remained no trace of blood.

He had long become immune to sleepless nights, but Kettering's memory would retain that one as the most harrowing. More harrowing than the one following Viola's tragedy.

Viola. His eyes wandered from his cup of weak tea to their wedding portrait on the sideboard. Viola, the student nurse who came to him as a temporary summer assistant and remained to become his wife. Tender, delicate Viola who soon blended into the Harborford way of life. He could see Laura now, a week after Viola had been washed overboard and all hope of recovering the body abandoned, standing at the edge of the cliff and fielding a small wreath of button roses into the waves beneath, gently reminding him after the wind-up and pitch, 'She always loved button roses.'

How long after this had he realised he was in love with Laura? Two Sundays later at a cocktail party at the Welbecks, when Emaline Welbeck, seeking to console the bereaved widower, had patted him gently on the back and said, 'Ed, you come up and look at her statue anytime you like' and Laura mistook the thoughtful gesture as callous cruelty and said so.

Viola.

Laura.

He reached for a bottle of brandy and poured some into the tea. He looked into the cup and saw Clive Fuller swearing him to an oath of secrecy about the event at the cottage. As though he could ever betray Laura. But whom did she murder and why? He'd witnessed some of Laura's violent fits of temper, but never once believed she could prove fatal to anyone. And in the same moment recalled tender, delicate Viola invading the chicken coop in the back yard, catching and decapitating a cockerel with the bland detachment of a manicurist scissoring a thumbnail.

For three weeks he forced himself to keep from phoning Dr Flint's sanatorium to inquire after Laura's condition. As far as Harborford knew, Laura had been attacked by a prowler and taken to London to recover. True, the Harborford grapevine which nurtured on a nourishment all its own had now embellished 'attack' with 'rape' and sundry, colourful conjectures as to the identity of the assailant. But most important, 'murder' had not been mentioned. How could it be mentioned if no body has been found? And if it has, it's Harborford's best-kept secret in over four centuries.

*Laura! Laura! If you'd asked Arthur for a divorce and married me, this never would have happened!*

Lonely, that's what I am, lonely and worried, and that's why I'm having such trouble with inspiration this morning.

Auriol Kendall sat on a camp stool facing a square of canvas on the easel, balancing a palette in her left hand, scratching her head with the wooden end of the thin brush she held in her right hand. Her greetings card company wanted more daffodils, but she wasn't in a daffodil mood, besides which, she was low on yellow ochre and didn't feel like driving into town for any. The art gallery stocked supplies mostly for her.

A butterfly made a three-point landing on the easel and Auriol growled. Fiona. Not a bloody word in over bloody three weeks and that's a hell of a way to treat the woman who's looked after and supported you most of your adult years. Taking off without so much as a by-your-leave in the middle of the night. It had to be the middle of the night, I never heard her driving off. She knows I sleep as though I was drugged and I still think I *was* drugged. That cup of Ovaltine she brought me after I got into bed that Sunday night tasted stronger than usual, though she insisted my taste buds were dead from all those martinis. It takes more than seven doubles to flatten Auriol Kendall and I only had seven, and I'm positive Fiona matched me double martini for double martini, why else the blistering argument?

Auriol groaned, placed the palette and brush on the grass at her feet, dug a pack of cigarettes from her bag and lit one. She blew smoke at the butterfly which held its ground. She wondered if there was such species as homing butterflies.

'Any messages?' she asked the insect coyly. It remained in position and she wondered briefly if it would remain there long enough for her to capture it on canvas.

'That's where butterflies belong!' she raged into the void, 'on canvas, not pinned under glass!'

Bloody Fiona, always free with her advice but never taking any. Auriol placed her right elbow on her right knee and cupped her chin. Fiona gone, and *Laura* gone. Attacked by a prowler. Auriol snorted. More than likely it was one of her boyfriends. The tease. If you ask me, she's been asking for rape the way she flirts with every available man in the village. Oh Emaline Welbeck can insist Laura doesn't flirt intentionally, but that's because Emaline castrated her brother Frank years ago and knows he's safe from any creatures of prey. Ahhh, Laura's not such a bad girl. She's a hell of a lot more fun since she sent that dreary Arthur to

54

Coventry. Of course Fiona didn't think he was all that dreary. Fiona never thinks *anyone* is all that dreary, but Fiona's a born nun. I should have left her in the convent, but by Christ she's all I've got now and I mean to hold on to her.

'Where the hell *is* she?' she shouted at the sky. She usually sent a postcard or two, and on two occasions there was the bonus of a phone call, charges reversed. But this time, sneaking away in the dead of night the way she did, she's never done anything like *that* before. True, that *was* a *blitzkrieg* of an argument we'd had, and maybe I *was* being unreasonable and selfish, but she didn't deny *any* of my accusations.

Auriol stroked her chin thoughtfully. I wonder if she's in Wales. That Professor Whatsisname and his wife have been bombarding her with invitations for months to join them on that field trip in the north to track another of those damned rare species. Now what was that postmark on their letters? Bryfflyrth? Wruglbthrb? Damn Wales. Auriol was convinced the name of every town in Wales was an anagram for something dirty. Fiona, Auriol finally decided, could be anywhere. Her red Volvo with the equipment she always kept in the boot was gone, and Fiona was gone, and Auriol was worried and lonely.

Her thoughts returned to Laura. I'll bet it was Sean who attacked her with a grappling hook. Certainly not mild Ed Kettering. The heart on his sleeve must be shrivelled from exposure.

The butterfly took off and Auriol was engulfed by a new wave of melancholia. The world is passing me by and I'm only just past fifty. I create inoffensive little water colours and they are my only communication to the world. My little paintings travel across the world by the thousands bearing messages of good cheer, messages of good cheer to everyone but their creator. The cigarette dropped from her fingers to the grass and she very sensibly ground it to oblivion with the heel of her very sensible shoe. Sensible

55

Auriol. A sensible marriage at the age of eighteen to a sensible army major who treated her with insensible insensitivity. But what was he *really* like, Fiona would ask Auriol when she first came to live with her. Sidney? Why Sidney was just an old-fashioned boor and martinet who darkened my life until I learned to brighten it in private with water colours. Did he die heroically in battle? Fiona eagerly asked, then displaying the first signs of her incurably romantic nature. No dear, he was fatally bitten by a black widow spider and his dying words, bless Sidney, were, 'It's always a woman.'

It's always a woman. Auriol's right leg shot out feroiciously and sent the easel crashing. 'Damn you, Fiona!' she sobbed into her open hands, damn you and damn women like Laura Denning who unlike me have the courage to attempt to renew life when they see it on the verge of withering. That's what you've done, Fiona, you're not off chasing butterflies, you're out there somewhere chasing life. Unlike me sitting here on this miserable, uncomfortable little camp stool which each day seems to grow too small for my ever enlarging backside, giving life to canvas but never to myself.

Auriol leapt to her feet and gave the camp stool a vicious kick. 'I shall have one last affair!' she roared, knowing full well the statement was as empty as the field through which it echoed. She hung her head, not in shame but with remorse for her impotence. Who would want me? She thought for a moment, then raised her head slowly, wiping her eyes with the backs of her hands, like the new child in the neighbourhood rejected on her first day in the playground.

Someone *seemed* to want me not too long ago. Perhaps it's not too late. Poke at a dying ember long enough, it sometimes catches fire. What was it Laura Denning had said to her months ago during a stroll along the cliffs by way of explanation for leaving Arthur?

'I've learned this, Auriol. Trying to make the best of a

bad deal is a waste of time, and time is something we have less of the older we get. Dying branches can't bear fruit.'

Auriol was walking slowly to her cottage, head thrust forward, hands behind her back with fingers interlocked in a grip a wrestler would envy, dwelling on Laura Denning. To Auriol Kendall, Laura Denning seemed to be a woman who had everything, so why did she want more? Why was she so positive it was Laura who was responsible for Fiona's slowly weaning herself away from Auriol's over-powering influence?

She chuckled to herself. How well does Laura *think* she knows Fiona? How would she react if I repeated the details of our awful argument that Sunday night? What would she think of Fiona's last threat before storming into the kitchen to make the Ovaltine. 'She'd better not stand in my way! Nobody had better stand in my way including *you*, Auriol. I'll *kill* anyone who does!'

Many Thursdays past, when the *Atlantis* was riding at anchor five miles offshore and the wind was wreaking havoc with Laura Denning's hair as she struggled to swallow the revulsion she always felt when slipping a fish hook through a wriggling worm, Sean Coleridge confided a secret to her.

'I hate the sea.'

Instead of launching into the editorial he usually expected of her, she had asked with genuine concern why he didn't try exploring another profession.

'I tried for over a year after leaving the merchant marine, a variety of jobs, but I wasn't much good at anything.'

'I know,' said Laura, following a grunt as she cast her line into the water, 'I loathe writing. I can't bear my sweaty palms when I'm struggling for fresh adjectives and I dread that awful exhaustion that follows five hours at the type-writer, but writing is all I can do well ... besides making a husband miserable.'

He remembered starting a gesture towards her hair where

57

the wind had made it resemble a curtain of fine threads, and then just as suddenly withdrew his hand when her eyes briefly met his and semaphored the message 'No Trespassing'. Instead he said for the tenth time that afternoon, 'I love you.'

'Yes, I know you do!' she shouted as her fishing line began to whirr on the reel, 'But save it for later! I've got a *bite*!'

He never told her that he realised then those nine words would always be to him the sum of Laura Denning. *But save it for later! I've got a bite.* He'd heard them before, the first time they'd gone to bed together in his isolated cabin on the beach. He remembered how the corners of her mouth had dropped at the room's untidiness and she wondered when he had last changed the sheets on the bed and was he sure there wasn't bedbugs? And when at the height of his passion she suddenly shrieked and certainly not with ecstasy, 'Save it for later! I've got a bite!'

He never admitted his jealousy when she shared her time with Ed Kettering, Frank Welbeck and sometimes Fiona Cooper. But he was fiercely jealous and when drunk even harboured dark thoughts of murder. He once jokingly offered to murder Arthur by throwing him overboard, but the joke never bore repetition, having been made the morning of the day Viola Kettering perished. Arthur saved him the trouble anyway by docilely permitting himself to be tucked away in Laura's dead letter file.

Coleridge listlessly stared around the deck at the six members of the day's fishing party, all seemingly frozen at the rail with rods in hand, reminding him of his favourite vaudeville act as a child, Living Statues. *Can I face this for the rest of my life without Laura?* He found a square of chewing tobacco in his trouser pocket and bit off a piece, began pulverising it with strong teeth then leaned over the rail, occasionally polluting the water with a stream of brown juice.

He worshipped Laura, and like the goddess he knew her

to be, it was fitting Frank Welbeck immortalise her in bronze, even though he envied and resented the time Laura had to give the sculptor. But Welbeck had stopped working on Charlotte Corday. Laura's misfortune had brought this piece of the project to a halt. Welbeck couldn't work without Laura, he told him that the previous evening at the bar of the Grace and Favour.

*Laura's misfortune.*

What was the truth of it? Attack, prowler, shame, detective, questions, will Laura ever return?

From his cabin that Sunday afternoon he'd seen Laura and Fiona walking on the beach and they'd seemed embroiled in a heated discussion, perhaps an argument. Should he have told that to Fuller? But to him it bore no relationship to what he was told happened to Laura later in her cottage, and so withheld the information. Anyway, Laura was always debating, or arguing, or lecturing. Why even poor Viola had been Laura's target on this very boat an hour before the storm broke, and he'd seen Emaline Welbeck eavesdropping, which was often unavoidable on a boat as small as the *Atlantis*.

He suddenly groaned inwardly. Laura's back in London with Arthur. They've been together for over three weeks. Is that enough time to effect a reconciliation? It had better not, he thought with black determination, clenched fists and a cascade of juice into the water, it damned well better not, or the next time he sets foot on this boat, *I'll push the scurvy bugger overboard!*

'*Drop that hammer!*'

Emaline Welbeck came tearing out of the house at full gallop screeching like a vulture circling a carcass, one hundred yards behind her younger brother, who with upraised arm holding a hammer, was drunkenly bearing down on the first of the five plaster of paris statues lining the driveway. They were to be recast in bronze when his ambitious project was completed but it was now apparent Frank Welbeck meant to shatter this ambition into smithereens.

'*Frank!*' she screamed. '*Frank!*'

Welbeck's face was an exaggerated mask of hatred. His tall, gaunt frame was tilted at a sixty degree angle, his weapon-bearing arm making ferocious circles, like David about to unleash the rock from his slingshot.

Emaline accelerated and began to gain ground as Welbeck neared Marie Antoinette.

'*Don't punish me like this Frank!*' she screamed, 'You're only punishing *yourself*! *Fraaaaannnnkkkkk!*'

With one powerful, desperate lunge, she leapt and went sailing through the air with arms outstretched, caught her brother around the hips, and they landed on the ground, Frank face downward in the grass, and Emaline nimbly scrambling to a sitting position on his back as she clawed at his right hand in an effort to wrest the weapon from his fingers. Welbeck howled a mixture of anger and pain, pouring his energy into his left hand which beat a merciless tattoo on Emaline's awkwardly outstretched left leg.

'Get off me, *Medusa*!' he bellowed, 'or I'll bash your skinny skull in!'

'*Let go of that hammer!*'

Welbeck twisted his head to the left as he brutally pulled his sister's leg towards him and finally mouth and calf connected.

'*Yiiiii!*' howled an agonised Emaline as she relaxed the grip on the hammer and pummelled his head with her strong fists. Mustering his remaining strength, Welbeck sent his sister sprawling on her back. He got to his knees, then with a further effort to his feet, and now towered over his cowering, weeping sister. He raised the hammer menacingly.

'Now, Medusa ... *Now!*'

Auriol Kendall, assisted by the malacca walking stick she favoured on her daily constitutional, was approaching the

Welbeck driveway when the first agonised cry of *'Help!'* zeroed in on her ears. She froze on the road, staring haphazardly in all directions, not quite sure where the cry had been launched.

*'Fraaaannnkkkkk! Nooooooo!'*

'Emaline!' gasped Auriol and took off at a trot towards the driveway.

*Whack!*

Auriol froze again. It sounded like an axe cutting into a treetrunk. Then her feet began to move again and in seconds she reached the perimeter of the vast expanse of green surrounding the Welbeck mansion.

'Oh my God,' she whispered. 'Oh my God, no.'

She saw Frank Welbeck swaying like a reed in a breeze, clutching a hammer in his right hand, near the furthermost of the five statues in her line of vision. At Frank's feet sat Emaline sobbing bitterly. Resting against Emaline's feet was a plaster of paris head.

Marie Antoinette had been decapitated again.

Chapter Six

'Isn't it possible *our* blood-stained victim left the cottage *alive*?'

Fuller privately enjoyed the subtle implication of togetherness in her use of the words *'our* blood-stained victim'. He needed her trust and cooperation. Fuller's Law, which he had put into effect some twenty years earlier, was to win the suspect's confidence, and he always treasured and made use of the trophy when handed to him.

'Well *isn't* it?' Laura pressed impatiently. She didn't care a fig how many more centuries the Sphinx kept its silence, but her life depended on Clive Fuller, and life was something she had every intention of holding on to.

'There was no trail of blood to the door,' he reminded her.

'People have been carried out of places before!' she insisted, counterpointing the statement with a scooping motion of her hands.

'There'd still be a trail of blood,' he insisted adamantly.

'Even if wrapped in a coat or a blanket or whatever was handy?' She folded her arms self-confidently and continued. 'The victim, dead *or* alive, was removed from the premises. It had to be wrapped in *something*!' The sly look on his face stopped her. 'Of course,' she said with chagrin, 'you've already mulled this one over.'

'That's right. I'll tell you one of my theories, but it's strictly between us.' She crossed her heart in an elaborate pantomime. 'I think there could have been at least two other people present in the cottage besides yourself and the victim, people you knew and trusted. There was a violent argument over something I pray God you will soon remember. The knife was probably quite handy on the table. When it was picked up someone interfered, which explains the struggle. Now the victim undoubtedly had a chance to flee, but didn't, so that means the victim was positive the assailant would be overcome.' Laura nodded vigorously as she mentally pictured the scene. 'Obviously, the victim was wrong. The blade was thrust,' Laura winced, 'and the victim fell back against the stove, then reeled against the wall adjoining the stove, and I'm positive it's at this point in the sequence of events you went into shock. I also think that was only the first stage of the crime.

'Next, I think, the assailant either dropped the knife on the floor or placed it back on the table, now sanely realising both the enormity of the crime and your cataleptic state. There *has* to be a close bond between the assailant and the other person I'm presuming was present in order for this other person to become a willing accomplice. It is this person who I think removed the body. The assailant, probably alone with you for a few moments after the victim was taken from the cottage, thought quickly and put the knife in your hand and then left.'

Laura was both perplexed and indignant. 'But why implicate me? Why ... why ... this person must *loathe* me!'

'I think so,' said Fuller quietly after striking a match, 'I also think the knife blade was originally meant for you.' He applied the match to the tobacco, seemingly oblivious to the fact that Laura might either faint or return to a cataleptic state. She did neither. She simply raised her right thumb to her mouth and deep in thought, gnawed at a cuticle, which occupied her for about fifteen seconds.

'I suppose I didn't run from the kitchen because whatever state of rage that person was in, I didn't for one minute think them capable of murder ... and was I ever wrong. *That's* what probably sent me into shock, the realisation the knife *was* meant for me!'

'Exactly.'

'In my now completely defenceless state, by what miracle do you suppose I was spared?'

'By a nasty piece of cold, albeit illogical thinking. And most crimes of passion are completely illogical. Out of perversely blind hatred, the knife was placed in your hand. When and if you came to your senses clutching the knife, no doubt strongly claiming your innocence, there would be two people to refute your statement. The assailant, like most people, probably has little knowledge of catalepsy and didn't recognise your state. That action also convinces me the victim was very dead when removed from the cottage.'

'But why remove the body at *all*?'

'I think that was the accomplice's idea. Whoever he or she is, I honestly believe the motive was noble. Get rid of the body, clear the kitchen of all trace of the crime, and hope when you revive you'd share their silence until something could be done about the assailant quietly and without scandal. After the body was disposed of, our vengeful assailant undoubtedly confided the knife was now in your hand, and before the accomplice could do anything about correcting that, Arthur arrived at the cottage.'

'Damn Arthur!' she snapped.

'*You* phoned him.'

'Damn me.'

'There's something else.' Her head shot up. 'You had an overnight guest. One of the other bedroom's had been slept in. There was also an unsigned, typewritten note in your dress pocket.' He blew a smoke ring and then told her, 'It said, *Leave Harborford or I'll kill you.*'

'Oh God,' she groaned, 'what awful thing have I done and to whom?'

'I think that's why you phoned Arthur rather than seek the aid of a local friend. Still want to go back?'

She thought for a moment, then thrust her chin forward and said, 'When do we leave?'

It was the first time he suppressed an urge to kiss her, not that her lips were unusually seductive at the moment. They were tightly pressed together with the determination of a small boy facing an unscaleable tree laden with ripe apples. 'Can't say yet when we'll be able to leave,' he said matter-of-factly.

Laura challenged him with spirit. 'We should leave at once! The first thing in the morning! There's a killer at large growing smug and complacent. . . .'

'. . . and frightened,' he interjected.

'Of course,' she agreed, 'frightened enough to be planning a bolt!'

'No,' he said calmly, 'there's the accomplice to consider. If my theory is right, that's the person I'm depending on to help break this case, unless your memory comes back. The killer has to stay put while there's the threat of the accomplice's knowledge.'

'There could be another murder.' She might have been auditioning for Lady Macbeth.

'We need to set the stage for your return to Harborford,' he told her, winning her undivided attention. 'In a day or two, I'd like you to write notes to your friends there. The usual thing, on the road to recovery, hoping to be back soon, all physical traces of your attack having more or less disappeared except one ... complete loss of memory from the shock, with the doctors holding little hope of your ever remembering.' She felt like an idiot as she realised she was bouncing up and down with enthusiasm. 'For added emphasis, you'll be returning with Arthur, a private nurse ...'

'Not *Murdock*!'

'A very capable woman. You'll then add by way of a postscript that you and Arthur and I have become so friendly, you've invited me to join me at the cottage as your guest for a few days.'

'That's about as subtle as rape.'

'It's meant to be.'

Fuller and I under the same roof in Harborford, she thought quickly, will that be as close as we ever get?

'Remember this,' she heard him saying, 'my theory is *only* a theory. I may be dead wrong. I've been wrong before.'

'Meaning possibly no accomplice?'

'I said I've been wrong before.'

What he wants to say but can't, she told herself, is that he might still end up proving I am a murderer. She next consoled herself that at her trial he'd make a fine character witness. 'When shall I send the notes?'

'I'll let you know in a few days. As soon as I've completed plans for your security there.'

Security for Laura. *Bait for the trap.* So this is how a heroine must feel in those Gothic thrillers I dip into when I can't fall asleep. 'Oh!' she said and Fuller jumped an inch. 'Sorry, but I just remembered something,' she said with delight and told him about dipping into Gothic thrillers.

'You're getting there,' he said.

'Will there be all sorts of plainclothes policemen swarming over the village?' she asked eagerly.

'Security is my department,' was all he said.

'Oh!' He jumped again. 'My handwriting!'

'What about it?'

'Supposing it's changed?'

He scratched his chin and then brightened. 'Arthur will write the notes for you.' She was glad Arthur could now be of some use. She had envisaged him sitting on the sidelines either expressing disapproval or keeping the score.

'I think I'll buy some new clothes.'

This was the second time he suppressed an urge to kiss her. He made a move to leave.

'Don't we have lots more to talk about?' she pleaded.

'There's tomorrow and the next day and it's late and my dinner's waiting.'

'Of course,' she said glumly, 'your dinner . . . uh . . . your family . . .'

'I'm a bachelor.' She tried not to brighten too visibly. 'Dinner with friends.'

'Oh well then,' she chirruped, 'hearty appetite!'

The next morning Laura decided to start a journal and sent Nurse Murdock scurrying for notebooks and pencils. For five days Doctor Flint and his staff gave her little time to make entries. There were a series of tests, examinations and head X-rays that brought her back to her room completely exhausted. There were dutiful daily visits from Arthur in the morning and late afternoon sessions with Fuller. Nurse Murdock was a perfect nuisance about what she ought to pack and Laura laid emphasis on hot water bottles. On the sixth day Arthur painstakingly wrote the notes dictated by Laura who had drafted them earlier with Fuller as editor. On the seventh day she did not rest, but, accompanied by Nurse Murdock and a young detective named Brian Cummings who had a shock of blazing red hair, she treated herself to a new wardrobe.

On the eighth day, after another series of tests, Dr Flint pronounced her eyesight completely back to normal which she refrained from admitting had occurred eight days earlier.

He pronounced her physically fit and was elated when she was able to remember her recipes for Long Island Meat Loaf and Eggs Laura. The doctor could now assure her there was no brain damage other than to the memory cells but these were obviously beginning to repair themselves, and she didn't dare to admit she was secretly dreading recovering her memory.

On the ninth day, which was a Saturday, Fuller announced Monday as zero hour, the return to Harborford. She experienced a sudden sensation of fear, her skin going clammy, but never admitted it to Fuller and instead spent a sleepless night.

Fuller sensed exactly how she felt, which was exactly the way he wanted it.

On Friday morning Auriol Kendall awoke with another splitting hangover. She staggered through morning ablutions and coffee, and then succumbed to a weeping fit. After two cigarettes and a shot of brandy she finally came to a decision to report Fiona Cooper missing to the police. Her world was falling apart, not the private world within the confines of her cottage, but her small world of Harborford. Fiona was gone. Laura was gone and her dreadful experience with Frank and Emaline Welbeck a week earlier still made her hands tremble at the memory of it.

'*Assassin!*'

Emaline's hysterical accusation to her brother as she pointed at Marie Antoinette's head still echoed in her mind. She'd never forget the look of hatred on Frank's face, as though etched there with acid, as he turned and stumbled back to the house, still clutching the hammer. The following fifteen minutes were equally unnerving, helping Emaline to her feet with what she hoped were appropriate soothing noises while all the time preoccupied with thoughts of the defected Fiona. Then guiding the near-limp woman back to her house and into the kitchen, placing the kettle on to boil and taking a moment to decide Emaline was a lousy

67

housekeeper. Frank had probably sequestered himself in his studio behind the house, the converted barn which was no-man's-land to everyone but Frank and whoever was modelling for him, the key always kept in his right hand trouser pocket.

Emaline, Auriol thought, was sobbing loud enough to shatter glass. The moment Auriol set the cup of tea in front of the unhappy woman, she announced her departure for the village, but Emaline's sobs increased in volume and the exasperated Auriol, feeling as martyred as a spinster daughter with an invalid mother, poured a cup for herself and then went hunting in the larder for some boiled sweets which she found and popped into her mouth like peanuts. Emaline's body heaved with emotional convulsions and for a moment Auriol feared the woman might shake her skin loose.

'There, there, dear,' said Auriol as she crunched down on a sweet and then sipped some tea.

'I live in terror!' exclaimed Emaline, 'stark dread terror. He's changed, he's changed terribly since Laura left!'

'He's an artist, dear,' said Auriol who as an artist felt she knew whereof she spoke, 'and without Laura he can't complete Charlotte Corday. It's perfectly *dreadful* when a work in progress is interrupted. Remember the hell I went through with those gladioli when the blight struck before I could finish the canvas?'

Emaline sympathised and then launched into a tirade against her brother with a catalogue of his shortcomings, the sum total of which nulled and voided his genius as a sculptor. Auriol had heard most of it before, but this was the first time in context. She hoped Frank wouldn't enter and demand equal time, she wanted to resume her walk to the village and think in private.

'But this drinking,' Emaline persisted, 'he starts in the morning and never lets up until he collapses at night!' On this score Auriol was allied with Frank but wisely decided this was not the time to say so. 'Now he wants to destroy everything ... *everything!*' She pushed her chair back, jumped to her feet and began pacing the room. 'I'm afraid, Auriol. I'm afraid. These statues were to be his legacy to the world, the heritage of his genius!' It sounded to Auriol like a funeral eulogy and made her uncomfortable. 'You *saw* what he did to Marie Antoinette? *Wham!*' Emaline's right hand made a wild arc like a scythe attacking a wheat field and Auriol ducked in time to avoid a clout in the ear. 'It's a good thing you came along, Auriol. He'd have smashed them *all* to bits.' She was studying the worn linoleum on the floor. 'Maybe he's calmed down now. Maybe he's come to his senses.' She crossed to a window and stared out at the studio several hundred yards away. 'It's quiet there. He's probably gone to sleep.' Auriol was out of her chair as Emaline came to her and squeezed her left arm. 'Thank you, Auriol. Thank you, and please, not a word of this to anyone.'

'Of course not, dear,' said Auriol, an easy thing to agree to as Frank Welbeck's dark moods were legend and had long ago become a bore.

She left Emaline standing alone in the centre of the kitchen, content to return to her own dark thoughts of Fiona.

Auriol's memory of the Welbeck incident dissolved like the glass of bromo seltzer she now held in her hand. She downed the concoction, grimaced, placed the glass in the kitchen sink then marched through the house to the front hall where she found her cape, deerstalker hat and walking stick. When everything was in place, she left the house and trudged heavily down the walk to the front gate and the mailbox. She found a note from Arthur Denning, tore the envelope open, read the brief message greedily then stuffed it in a pocket and leaned against the gate, thinking.

*Laura has suffered complete loss of memory.*

And Arthur is returning with her to Harborford. And a private nurse. And that Fuller person as their guest.

*Fuller! He'll* be the one to tell about Fiona! I'll wait for

Fuller. It's only another few days. I can survive that. I might even hear from Fiona by then instead of making a damn fool of myself by turning her in as a missing person. What she had actually thought was 'juvenile delinquent' though Fiona was over thirty. It made her think of the Welbecks again. Frank and Emaline. Auriol and Fiona. Emaline treats Frank like her child. *I do the same with Fiona.*

Oh dear Lord. Dear dear Lord. Fiona! Is that why you've fled? Have you discovered the *truth*?

Edmund Kettering read Arthur's note in the surgery, and let out a yell of joy. 'Laura!' And then just as swiftly, his mood darkened. Arthur. Laura and Arthur are coming back together. And a private nurse. And Fuller. Arthur wrote the note, not Laura. She can't be completely well.

*Laura has suffered complete loss of memory.*

He crossed slowly to his desk and sank into the chair. Complete loss of memory. Memory of *what*? He leaned forward in the chair, hands clasped between his legs. A portion of the crumpled note in his hands projected from between two fingers and he relaxed his hands, smoothed out the paper and read again what was written there. Search as he could, he discerned nothing between the lines. The message was straightforward. Why hadn't Laura written it herself? Because with loss of memory she wouldn't trust the authenticity of her handwriting. My poor Laura. How you must be suffering! Have you been told everything? The state of the kitchen that morning, the blood-stained knife clutched in your hand.

They must have told you. Why else would Fuller be returning with you. He sat up with a start. I wonder. Is it possible? It must be. Fuller has also fallen under your spell! Oh no . . . no! Not another rival.

You belong to *me*, Laura, and I mean to have you! Arthur's returning with you can only be a pose. Fuller's returning with you is undoubtedly cloaking further investigation. It's me you want to see. *Me!*

Loss of memory. My darling Laura . . . do you remember *me*?

Sean Coleridge re-read Arthur's note for the fifth time, his lips moving silently as they always did when he read. Gulls screeched overhead and water lapped against the hull of the boat. Somewhere on the ship he heard one of his crew singing a bawdy song and from another section of the boat he heard hammering. Sean looked up from the note and stared out at the sea.

*Loss of memory.* Arthur. Private nurse. Fuller. Damn! There'll be no getting her to the cabin for weeks, maybe months, and his body ached for hers. Fuller, and the train of thought on his one-track mind was derailed. Why was Fuller coming back, and as their *guest*?

He placed the note in his shirt pocket and then clutched the rail of the boat with both hands, the knuckles showing white. What he had been suspecting was true. They knew there was more to that story of an attack by a prowler. It was all too pat, too simple, and in a sense too ordinary, and ordinary things didn't happen to Laura Denning because Laura Denning was no ordinary woman.

The village has been whispering 'rape' but if any woman was capable of parrying a sexual assault, it was Laura Denning. He knew. His jaw ached and his shins showed bruises just reminding himself of the first time he'd tried it. Laura Denning wasn't a woman you raped. You learn it's simpler to just proposition her brazenly and, just as brazenly if the mood suits her, the palm is yours. Ed Kettering isn't telling all he knows. Since that day he was called to Royalties he's been moody, sullen, dejected and uncommunicative. He'd heard patients after visiting Kettering's surgery complaining the doctor didn't make bad jokes anymore. They needed the doctor's bad jokes. It gave them confidence his ministrations would have to be an improvement.

Laura had persistently denied any romantic relationship

with Kettering at the same time reminding him even if there was, it was none of his damned business. 'I'm not about to get seriously involved with anyone. I've spent the past eight years living between parentheses, but I'm in no rush to ask Arthur for a divorce.' In his mind he could see her clearly when she spoke those words, sitting in the lounge of the Grace and Favour late one wintry evening, the burning fireplace pale in comparison to the flame in Laura's face.

Laura was never in a rush about anything. She was painstakingly slow and meticulous in both her work and her relationships. Coleridge had to admit this to himself, anything Laura erected had a solid foundation. He could never say the same about himself. Even his boat never stopped rocking. But deep emotion was something new to him. He'd never had to cope before and there was no manual available in the Do-It-Yourself series.

He reclaimed the note from his pocket and studied it again, his lips moving like a sorcerer incanting a silent spell. A fresh breeze caused the paper to flutter and he relaxed his grip. The paper sailed away, making small orbits until it landed in the water and he dug into a pocket for his chewing tobacco.

Alone in his studio, Frank Welbeck was slowly circling Charlotte Corday. Charlotte certainly needed a lot more work and he'd been wondering if he could finish her from memory. Emaline would never realise that his violent decapitation of Marie Antoinette that awful morning had served to return his senses. She was too busy sobbing herself to see the tears in his eyes when Marie's head came to rest at Emaline's feet, the plaster of paris eyes in Frank's sodden state suddenly appearing to take on life, staring up at him in a mixture of sorrow, reproval and disappointment. Later that night, he'd stolen out and carefully repaired the damage, and the next day, Emaline was careful to reserve comment on the resurrection.

*Twelve infamous women in history.*

After Charlotte Corday, Frank thought wearily, six more to go. Would there be time? How could he have permitted his monumental ego to drive him into this project? For Rodin, it would have been a lifetime's work, for Welbeck, twelve years. *Twelve years.* For some, Frank consoled himself, that's a lifetime. Progress had gone steadily on his first five subjects, even with the two professional models he'd used for Marie Antoinette and Cleopatra, despite the torrid affairs he'd had with both of them and the accompanying emotional tensions, mostly Emaline's. Then to assuage Emaline, he shrewdly persuaded her to pose for Lucrezia Borgia, and it proved to be a happy marriage of model and subject, probably the only time in her life Emaline would know a successful liaison.

Welbeck sat on a wooden crate and stared at Charlotte Corday.

*Marie Anne Charlotte Corday d'Armans (1767–1793), a French patriot who assassinated Marat in Paris July 13, 1793, and was guillotined.*

'*Off with her head!*' he whispered, and then shook his own head sadly. How do I finish her, he wondered. Not when, but how? She's not what I intended at all. Even from simple-minded, ill-starred Viola Kettering the Catherine de Medici he'd always envisioned emerged successfully. Fiona's Sappho was truly a thing of beauty, as much from Fiona's immersing herself in research on the lady as from his own artistry. But Charlotte Corday was all wrong. She seemed as distorted as the interpretation given her character by most historians. *Assassin!* How ironic of you, Emaline, how truly ironic. You who are my slow, lingering death.

He was circling Charlotte Corday again. This isn't Charlotte Corday at all. It isn't even Laura Denning, what do I do? I am a perfectionist, a genius (his chest expanded slightly as he thought this), can I permit this one lapse in my creative ability, this piece of slipshod construction to

73

represent me for posterity?

'*You can fix her up! You know you can, Frankie! You can fix anything!*' Was that the voice of Emaline the adult or Emaline aged twelve tearfully begging the younger brother to repair a broken doll.

I'll fix it up, Emaline. You know me in the face of a challenge. Don Quixote tilting at windmills. I'll fix you up, Charlotte Corday. God knows how but I will. Will Laura ever sit for me again? Can I ever breathe life again into this dead creature? Aren't miracles denied atheists?

'Frank! *Fraaaank!*' From a distance, Emaline's voice pierced his reverie like a laser beam. 'Frank!' She was beating on the studio door.

'Go away!' he shouted at the door, 'I'm working! You know better than to disturb me when I'm working!' He crossed to his work desk and picked up a chisel.

'We have a note from Arthur!'

His fingers became rigid around the chisel.

'Do you hear me, Frank? Arthur's written to us! They're coming *back*!'

Frank made it to the door in six long strides, unbolted and opened it. Emaline stood there clutching a sheet of stationery, her eyes blinking wildly, her left hand pressed against her meagre chest, her lower lip quivering. Frank held his hand out and she gave him the note. He scanned it rapidly, then turned and slowly crossed back to the work table, Emaline shuffling behind him like an obsequious Chinese amah fearful of getting the sack.

When he reached the table he placed the note on it, holding it down with both hands.

'Well, *say* something!'

Over his shoulder he glanced at his anxious sister. He moistened his lips, and then said very slowly, 'I wish you were dead.'

Chapter Seven

*Dear Diary*, Laura wrote in the notebook the evening of the day Arthur had written the brief letters to Harborford, 'the following is really none of your business, but why else keep a journal so here goes.'

*Dear Diary* looked as childish and immature to her as the unfamiliar scrawl she had now learned to accept as her handwriting, but who, she consoled herself, ever wrote *Dear Journal* unless as the heading of a letter to the editor?

*Clive Fuller is the most fascinating man I've ever met, until my memory returns and I recall other fascinating men before him, which is highly unlikely considering I stuck it out with Arthur all these years. For the past five days, he has arrived promptly at five in the afternoon for our daily talks and we are certainly learning more and more about each other. Today of course he came promptly at noon as it was prearranged with Arthur to be here and write the notes I dictated to the Welbecks, Auriol and Fiona, Doctor Kettering, Coleridge and the Vicar, whose name I couldn't remember of course but Fuller (bless him!) supplied that, Owen Farquhar. After Arthur left, Fuller remained to have lunch with me brought in by Nurse Murdock with her usual sickeningly cheery announcement, 'Din Dins everybody!'*

*Oh how slyly he reveals new information to me about the awful event! For instance he's convinced the person who spent the night at the house was a woman, as there was a faint scent of perfume lingering on the pillow. It certainly wasn't me as he checked mine and it didn't match. The strange scent, says Fuller, reminded him of heliotrope and I can't wait to get to a flower shop and smell heliotrope so I can recognise it. The kitchen was also completely wiped clean of fingerprints which was a serious error on the assail-*

*ant's part, as certainly MY fingerprints should have been all over the place. Fuller, bless him, doesn't think I'd have been stupid enough to do a thing like that which I couldn't have done in the first place as I was in my trance. We discussed the possibility of Arthur's having tried to be helpful and done the job himself but we ruled that out after I decided Arthur wasn't capable of thinking that quickly. The final cleaning-up of the mess in the kitchen was done by Doctor Kettering and the two local constables who have already been alerted to our imminent return.*

*Now then, apparently I did or do have a new book in progress. The Crippen case again, which has been hashed and rehashed a dozen times in print so why am I doing it again unless I have some startling new theories to offer which darling Fuller assumes I do. What I'm getting at, which seems terribly important to Fuller, is that when I'm working, according to Arthur, I'm impossible to be with, so if I was involved with someone in Harborford, I must have been giving that person a terribly hard time. Now I'm almost embarrassed to write the following, but Fuller tells me Sean Coleridge admits we've been having an affair and Edmund Kettering told him he's asked me to marry him time and again. My cup runneth over. And so what's with Frank Welbeck? Do my charms elude him as he's not all that old or is he too absorbed in his project to notice my fatal allure?*

*I questioned Fuller about footprints around the kitchen door but there too nothing. We have decided we are up against a very clever adversary (ies?).*

'Din Dins!' and that finished the journal for that day.

The following evening Laura wrote:

*Exhausted! My first day out of stir with Doctor Flint's permission. He's really an old dear. He never stops complimenting me on my X-rays. He makes my brain sound so lovely, I'm wondering if Cecil Beaton would like a go at it. Spent five hours shopping with Nurse Murdock and a cute young detective as bodyguards (or to make sure I didn't try to escape, hmmmm??). His name is Brian Cummings, with the reddest hair I've seen this side of Moira Shearer, but has an unfortunate nasal defect which I attribute to a deviated septum and if I ever see him again I shall subtly suggest corrective surgery as I think Nurse Murdock's getting a case on him and I can see him twenty years from now punchdrunk from those pounding Din Din's. When we got back, darling Clive was waiting and munching on his bloody pipe stem. He told me security has been arranged in Harborford but wouldn't give me the details. Loving a man with an air of mystery about him must be something new for me. There's certainly nothing mysterious about Arthur except why he loathes the thought of returning to Harborford with us. Or does he loathe the thought of possibly finding out I'm IT? I loathe it TOO!*

When she was two lines into the next night's entry, a fresh excitement boiled within her and she could barely contain herself until Fuller's next visit.

*Doctor Flint announced this morning my eyesight was in perfect shape again. I didn't have the nerve to admit I'd been shamming to everyone except Clive since the day I reawakened.*

Her handwriting was changing. It was no longer a childish, barely legible scrawl. There was a new strength in the consonants and a feminine grace to the vowels. She carefully checked this against the previous entry and couldn't be sure which belonged to Jekyll and which belonged to Hyde. That would be for a graphologist to decide if Fuller suggested they bring one in for consultation. Laura didn't think this would be necessary. The re-emergence of the true Laura Denning handwriting was in keeping with the pattern that had begun to establish itself earlier that day. It had occurred during a session of chit-chat with Nurse Murdock when she suddenly recalled two recipes which she was able to identify as Long Island Meat Loaf and Eggs Laura ('Jiffy dishes!' she had told the equally elated Nurse Murdock). She thought of tracking down Clive Fuller immediately to share her discovery, then reminded herself it wasn't as though she'd just invented the wheel. She also reminded herself that this was the beginning. The memory cells were repairing themselves.

How long would this go on, she wondered impatiently, teasing and tantalising herself with returning snippets of her old self. How will the final reconversion come about? Will I slip into another trance and then re-emerge with the name of my supposed lover on my lips and goodbye Clive Fuller? She didn't like the idea one bit. The return to Harborford now began to seem less an adventure and more a threat. She wrote that in the journal. If she did prove to be a murderer, she wanted written evidence for Clive Fuller of the sincerity of her deep feelings towards him.

The next day, which was Saturday, Clive Fuller arrived shortly after lunch and announced Monday for the departure to Harborford. She merely nodded like an attentive pupil anxious to retain her status as teacher's pet. Clive Fuller now knew and understood her too well to let her troubled expression go unnoticed.

'What's wrong?' he asked with concern.

'I want to show you something,' she said in a hoarse voice. She opened the journal to the first entry, masking with her hand all but the first sentence.

'Very amusing,' he commented dryly. She turned to a fresh page and wrote her name and address and then pushed it under his nose.

He studied the new page carefully and said, 'It's quite a difference.'

'Exactly.'

They were seated in comfortable chairs at the window, a coffee table separating them. The sunlight streaming into the room could not brighten Laura's dark mood.

'That's obviously my true handwriting and I'm frightened.'

'Why?'

'Because I'm beginning to be afraid of what I might remember.' She was out of the chair and pacing the room with arms folded, while Fuller mentally noted she was one of the few women he knew who looked good in trousers. 'And don't repeat your theory to salve my fears. You said you could be wrong and I have to consider that.' She stopped near the bed and faced him. 'If the truth when I remember it is that I've murdered someone, I think I'm going to lie through my teeth.'

'I don't think so,' he said with overexaggerated confidence. 'Keep this in mind. If you did commit murder, the chances are good it was self-defence.'

'You have a theory for everything, Mr Fuller. Have you accumulated a file to suit every occasion?'

'If it's any consolation, I've been discussing you for the past hour with Doctor Flint. The recipes you recalled yesterday. It's a drop in the bucket. It's going to take time, a lot more time than you think before the big ones start turning up.'

'Supposing the dam bursts the minute I set foot in the village.'

'We all make for the hills,' he said with a smile.

'Very funny.' She sat on the bed and contemplated her shoes and decided silver buckles were definitely not for her. She heard a match strike, smelled tobacco burning and glanced at Fuller. He was a study in relaxation and she realised then he was more than positively on her side. She hated needing reassurance and wondered to which Laura this feeling belonged. He also has a job to do, she reminded herself, and if I really care about this man, I have to help him find the solution. This realisation began to fill her with fresh strength. I do care about this man. I will help him.

'Oh the hell with it!' she shouted and the lighted match dropped to the floor. He stomped on it and she fell back on the bed laughing. When the laughter abated, he was standing over her. She struggled to a sitting position with her face positioned in a direct line to his chest and waited. He patted her cheek and returned to his chair with a brusque: 'Now let's get down to it. There's a lot to discuss before Monday.'

His fingers on her cheek, their first physical contact. Like the awaited return of her memory, everything was going slowly.

That Saturday afternoon Sean Coleridge's first mate, Billy Merkle, who looked and walked like a trained simian, ambled up the gangplank and told Coleridge the new fishing party had just checked into the Grace and Favour. Coleridge had been expecting a party of five from London.

'What are they like?' Coleridge asked.

'Young 'uns,' Billy told him. Sean knew that to Billy, anyone under forty was a 'young 'un'. 'Real young 'uns,' Billy emphasised. That meant thirty or under. Sean preferred that. Older parties tended to flag by mid-day and bring out the whisky hours before returning to port, which added hazards to the trip. Viola Kettering was the last person to fall overboard and he didn't relish a repetition of the incident. 'Look clean,' added Billy. That meant they were probably middle to upper class. Sean preferred that too. That meant they took their fishing seriously.

'Any women?'

'Nup.'

That was even better. Women along for the ride grew bored and restive and sometimes occupied themselves attempting to win Sean's attention. On several trips that had led to trouble, and there was enough troubling Sean. Laura was returning in two days and he wasn't sure when he'd be able to see her. He'd be at sea with his party until the evening, then there'd be another hour or two cleaning up the boat. It might be too late then to pay a call at Royalties. And what would the proper procedure be now at Royalties with Arthur, Fuller and a private nurse present?

'Ahoy there!'

He looked up sharply and saw the Vicar standing at the foot of the gangplank. The Vicar always reminded Sean of a shorter, beardless Santa Claus. He returned the greeting and invited Mr Farquhar aboard. They retired to Sean's cabin, and over glasses of whisky the Vicar explained his visit. He had just returned from his weekly call on Auriol Kendall and it was his impression that the woman distinctly was in need of help. Fiona had been gone almost five weeks now and Auriol had had no communication from her in all that time. Then the Vicar leaned forward conspiratorially, looked around with caution at a cabin that was barely roomy enough for the two of them and whispered, 'Miss Kendall is drinking a great deal.'

'Miss Kendall usually drinks a great deal,' Sean stated flatly.

'But it's worse,' said the Vicar, pulling a handkerchief from his back pocket and mopping his perspiring brow. 'She behaved most ... well ... *peculiarly*!' Sean shrugged and the Vicar continued with an obvious effort. 'Well to put it bluntly, lad, I believe she made advances towards me!'

Mr Farquhar lowered his eyes demurely while Sean spent several minutes choking on a mouthful of whisky. He finally managed to speak. '*Not* our Auriol?'

'Oh yes,' said the Vicar, 'and I've always looked upon her as a backbone of the community.' He took a sip of whisky and then continued. 'I must say, she was most ardent and when I made a move to leave, she stood at the door and barred my way! I suppose it's this business about Fiona, but the experience was most unsettling.' He mopped his brow again. 'I tried to reason with her, and ... and she accused me of ... oh dear ... of secretly fancying Laura Denning!' The glass headed for Sean's mouth froze in mid-air. 'Then she said terrible things about poor Laura. You know she'll be back on Monday?' Sean told him about his note from Arthur. 'Well ... now she threatens to face Mr Denning and tell him about all of poor Laura's affairs ... that is ... affairs she *thinks* Laura has been having.' Sean

81

remained silent. 'This puts me in such a delicate position. If the Dennings are reconciled, Auriol Kendall could spoil everything. I . . . I've come to you for advice, Sean, because you're one of the men Auriol accuses.'

'Auriol Kendall's a dried-up old bitch!' cried Sean, slamming his glass down and lurching to his feet. 'Ah! She'll sleep this off and then forget about the whole thing.'

'She won't,' said the Vicar sadly. 'She hints something worse happened to Laura than a prowler's attack, why else bring that Mr Fuller back here with her? Auriol became violent in both speech and action and I didn't know how to cope. You're my friend, Sean, more than just a member of the parish. Sean . . . *I struck her!*' He held up his right hand and stared at it with horror. Sean wedged his way on to the bunk next to the Vicar and put his arm around his shoulder. 'There's more, Sean. She . . . she collapsed. I left her lying there in the hall. I panicked. What shall I do? Please help me.'

Sean felt the Vicar trembling. His first thought was to jolly the little man. 'Well you know what Noel Coward once said, "Women should be struck regularly . . . like gongs." '

The Vicar replied weakly, 'That's all well and good for Mr Coward, he's musical.' He glanced at Sean. 'I've been the Vicar in this parish for twenty years with never a breath of scandal. If I'm dismissed, I have nowhere to go. Dear dear dear.' He was rubbing his hands together nervously. 'I never dreamt there was violence in me. I've never raised my hand before except to point the way to God.'

Sean patted the Vicar gently, then rose and crossed to the porthole. He was thinking of Auriol and Fiona, two women imprisoned by a mutual need for each other, whose sedentary existence seemed idyllic to the casual observer, as pastoral as a tropical island where in actuality the natives lived in fear of a dormant volcano. He turned back to the Vicar. 'She isn't *dead*, is she?'

'Oh, bless the Lord no!' cried the Vicar, 'she just crumpled in a heap with her eyes open staring at the ceiling, breathing quite heavily. I ... I suppose I should have helped her to her feet or brought her a glass of water ... but ... but I was afraid she would start *again* ... I went to Edmund's surgery first, but he was out on a call ... so I came to you ... you're so ... so worldly, Sean ... I ... I thought you might have had similar dealings before.'

Sean clapped a hand over his mouth to stifle the laughter about to erupt. He poured fresh drinks and the Vicar accepted his with alacrity. 'What was that you said?' asked Sean. The Vicar was mumbling.

'I said I think this incident might have been triggered by Fiona.'

'Fiona's not here.'

'No ... no ... let me explain. I've been counselling Fiona. She's a very unhappy, very disturbed young woman.' This wasn't news to Sean. 'You understand whatever Fiona's discussed with me is privileged information ... but ... but I *did* advise her to the best of my ability ... after all ... I'm a man of God but not of the world ... but ... *I* told her to go away ... I think Auriol knows that and resents me for it ... and ... and *deliberately* set the stage for this unfortunate incident. Auriol is a terribly *vengeful* woman ... Oh! May God forgive me.'

'God doesn't punish the truth,' said Sean calmly. 'Where did Fiona go?'

'I don't know! When I last saw her, which was the Sunday afternoon before she left, she gave me no indication she meant to leave immediately. In fact, she said something about seeking a second opinion. I think she intended to ask Laura's advice. He downed his drink and stared at the bottle with an Oliver Twist expression on his face. Sean poured the Vicar's third while he dwelled on Laura. All roads lead to Rome and to Laura. Was Fiona in some way connected with the incident at Royalties? Still holding the bottle, he returned to the porthole.

Laura. Fiona. Arthur. Detective. Auriol. Private nurse. He felt like a child at school again presented with another of the interminable word games that left him helplessly confused. He had never been any good at puzzles. The intelligence he had developed as an adult came from experience, not from instruction. But one thing he felt sure of, there was more to the Laura story than a prowler's attack.

*She has suffered a complete loss of memory.*

'Was there a man involved?'

'Where?' asked the startled Mr Farquhar.

*'Fiona!'* Sean spoke her name like a terminal illness. He didn't like Fiona the way he didn't like sugar in his tea. To Sean she was too sweet, too saintly, too apparently pure and he never understood, or even cared to take the time to examine closely the relish she took in netting and pinning butterflies.

'I've told you all I can about the poor lass,' said the Vicar sadly. 'What shall I do about Auriol?' he pleaded.

'Leave her lying there,' replied Sean as he moved away from the porthole shoving his hands into his pockets. 'You'll hear no more about this, I can assure you. She's probably feeling a perfect fool herself at the moment,' he said confidently.

'Oh dear, oh dear.' The Vicar struggled to his feet. 'I hope you're right.' Then he clasped his hands and raised his head with his eyes shut.

' "A woman scorned is a vessel of wrath." '

'Stop worrying about Auriol. She has strength, but not enough to rock a boat. No one would believe her anyway.'

'Why not?'

'You *are* the Vicar,' Sean reminded him.

The Vicar opened his eyes and unclasped his hands. He managed a smile of thanks, and then deeply preoccupied again, left the cabin.

Bloody Auriol. Bloody Fiona. Sean was pouring another drink for himself.

Bloody Laura?

Auriol Kendall staggered to the kitchen sink, with shaking hand ran the water tap, tore a dish towel from its hook, drenched it and applied it to her feverish brow.

'God have mercy,' she groaned aloud. 'Oh God have mercy ... *how* could I have sunk so *low*.' She sank into a chair and propped her elbow on the table. Two tiny trickles of water escaped the towel to join two tiny trickles of tears seeping from her eyes and made their way to the drooping corners of her mouth. She licked and caught them both, her tongue moving back and forth like a windscreen wiper. The towel slipped down her face and landed in her lap, the resultant dampness causing no discomfort as Auriol felt completely numb. She opened her mouth and a sigh escaped that caused cigarette ashes in a dish on the table to form a small black tornado.

'How ... *How* can I ever face him again?' Her shoulders heaved slightly as she reached for a jar of boiled sweets, unscrewed the cap and shook two into her hand. Her teeth welcomed them with the ferocity of a garbage disposal truck. As she chomped away, she reached a decision. Flinging the towel to the floor, she jumped to her feet, went in to the sitting room and barked a number into the telephone.

'This is the Vicarage,' she heard Mr Farquhar's unsteady voice sounding like a recorded announcement.

Auriol swallowed, cleared her throat, and then mustered a chirp. 'Ow ... *en*? Auriol!' She thought for a moment the phone dropped at the other end. 'Owen?' she barked.

'Oh my dear, my dear.'

'Owen!' she spoke the name with renewed vigour. 'As a servant of God, you must find it in your heart to forgive me.' She screwed up her face like an anxious pekinese. 'Forgiven?'

Owen Farquhar stared at his phone in relieved disbelief. Then squaring his shoulders, he spoke in the voice he usually reserved for Deutoronomy, 'My dear Auriol, we must find it in *our* hearts to forgive each other.'

'I have searched and I have found,' she said dramatically, 'and *oh* how I forgive. Bless you.'

'Bless you right back.' He replaced the phone and bounced in his chair with a buoyancy new to him. 'Randy bitch!' he shouted at the phone, 'you'll never get the facts out of *me*!'

The look of brave resolve on Auriol's face as she slammed the phone down would have elated a general sending his troops into battle. Owen knows all right Auriol said to herself, he knows why Fiona's left me. Privileged information indeed. He doesn't *have* to tell me. It's a *man*! Her flesh may be weak, but her spirit was certainly willing. What the Vicar knows, someone else knows. Without looking at the target she slammed her fist down on the table and howled in pain as it struck an edge.

Auriol raced back into the kitchen and held the smarting fist under the cold water tap, swiping at and connecting with the jar of sweets en route. Deep in equal proportions of thought and pain, she pulverised a fresh mouthful of sugared victims. Someone else knows and that someone else is Laura Denning.

*She has suffered a complete loss of memory.*

'I wonder,' she murmured to herself, 'I do indeed wonder.' Words held hands and danced around the imaginary maypole of her mind. Laura, Arthur, Fuller, Nurse, Edmund, Sean, Frank, Emaline, Vicar, Fiona, and Fiona tripped and lay there.

'Oh you wretched child!' she shouted to the empty kitchen, 'you wretched, wretched child!' and then burst into tears.

*'Help!'*

Laura shot bolt upright as though catapulted. The cry had awakened her and she was perspiring. It was the middle of the night, the room was in darkness, her body was trembling and she realised it was she who had shouted. It was a nightmare that had awakened her. A frightening, hideous nightmare. She groped for the night lamp and

86

found the switch. She saw her notebook and pencil, flipped to a clean page and started scribbling rapidly, pausing only to brush the hair back from her eyes. She was obsessed with recording as much of the dream as she could remember. She was positive it was significant, it had to be significant, because the last thing she remembered of the dream was blood-bathed floor and wall, a woman's agonised cry and a hand clutching a carving knife, and then the cry for help with which she had awakened herself.

Damn me for that, she admonished herself as she wrote, damn me ... I was about to see a face ... *a face* ... and I had to go and wake myself up! *Damn me!*

The pencil lead broke.


## Chapter Eight

Dame Marjorie Denning staring at her son Arthur across the rim of the tea cup from which she was sipping, could only see half his face. Her view emphasised his eyes which were pale and watery under furrowed brows encompassed by a desert of sallow skin. For the second time that morning, she was suppressing an overpowering urge to box his ears. She wasn't angry with Arthur, she simply found him to be a simple-minded unworldly bore, too much like his father before him. Ridding herself of Simon Denning had been a simple matter of packing clothes and child and emigrating from South Africa, but from the look of Arthur he seemed here to stay and she had no intention of abandoning her house to him.

The dynamic career in politics that followed her defection had been rewarded by his late Majesty, but it was small comfort for the booby-prize presented to her by Simon earlier. She'd given up ages ago trying to figure out which, if any, of her son's charms had won him Laura. She liked Laura because Laura was a great deal like herself, which gave her cause to shudder if that was what drew Arthur to Laura. Laura was clever, attractive, talented and witty, or at least *was* when Arthur first brought her back from America. She had suffered in silence Laura's metamorphosis after the marriage, a similar creeping death to the one she escaped by a hair's breadth when she abandoned Simon.

The day Arthur had finally admitted he and Laura were estranged, she'd considered sending her daughter-in-law a large bouquet of roses and a diamond clip but abandoned the thoughtful if frivolous gesture when her housekeeper reprimanded her for disloyalty to her son.

This morning was the first she'd learned of Laura's unfortunate experience at Royalties and the amnesia, and she had strangled a wicked urge to tell Arthur some women would go to unusual lengths to forget a husband. Instead, she admonished him for not telling her sooner. 'I should have visited her days ago,' she said in the voice so familiar to the House of Commons and television audiences.

'She wouldn't know you,' said Arthur morosely.

'Well then,' said his mother cheerfully, 'I could enjoy the pleasure of making friends with her again.' It then occurred to her that Laura didn't recognise the old Arthur either and might make the stupid mistake of falling in love with him again. She spoke the thought much more diplomatically but Arthur assured her such was not the case. 'Arthur?' she spoke his name sharply, 'are you still in love with Laura?'

Her son pulled at his nose and then said, 'There are times when I miss her terribly.'

'Have you been having an affair?' she asked briskly.

'What difference does *that* make? After all, Mother, I'm only human.'

Had he made that statement during a session at Parliament, she'd have risen with a strong rebuttal, but she reminded herself this was her son and tried to recall the feeling of maternal instincts. 'If you want her back you must fight for her.' He said nothing. 'Arthur, there's more to this unfortunate affair at Royalties, isn't there?' He covered his eyes with his hands and shifted in his chair and she wondered if she'd get results in a dark room with him under a glaring spotlight and she wielding a rubber truncheon. A second later she decided it wouldn't help. Arthur was too insensitive.

Why, he was wondering, had he bothered to come see the gargoyle. He couldn't tell her facts of what he'd found in the cottage because he'd been sworn to secrecy, and secrecy was the biggest part of Arthur's nature. But to some extent he *was* a bit human and he needed someone to talk to and this was as good an excuse as any to pay a duty visit.

She'd grown impatient with his silence. 'Oh come now, Arthur. There is more to it because if there wasn't, you'd have told me weeks ago Laura was in Flint's sanatorium and you wouldn't be here this morning. And why else would you, a nurse and a detective be accompanying her back to Harborford tomorrow?'

He found words. 'I simply wish to warn you, this all might result in newspaper headlines.'

'Ah. Well. Now then.' She brushed a biscuit crumb from her lap. 'And that's all you can tell me?'

'That's all. I'm sorry.'

'So am I. I suppose there's no way I can help?'

'No.' He had wanted to say, 'Yes ... be kind, sympathise, show warmth, I'm ice cold inside ...' but he'd felt none of this from his mother since the age of seven when he'd been packed off to school, and after his abandonment had become too shy and introverted to express his needs.

'Very well, Arthur,' he heard her say, 'forewarned is forearmed. Thank you for preparing me, and when shall I expect the deluge?'

His eyes were able to meet hers again. 'When Laura regains her memory, if not before.'

The tea cup was back at her lips and she wished he would go. She needed to think, to arm herself mentally against the invisible enemy, a possible scandal. There was nothing she could do for Arthur, which left the field all clear to herself. Stupid Arthur. I am a powerful woman with powerful allies. Doesn't he know I might be in a position to put a stop to all this? She thought of saying this, but then decided to bide her time when he announced his departure.

Put a stop to what, she puzzled as Arthur saw himself to the door. The heading of this curriculum is Scandal but what's the subject? She considered and discarded infidelity immediately. It was much too commonplace and it would have hardly caused Laura's amnesia or a police investigation. She crossed from her chair to the window overlooking the street and watched Arthur waiting for a taxi. Can't he ever remember to go to the top of the square where the traffic is heavier? He must be much more disturbed than he's let on. She raised the window and called out to him. 'Arthur! You'll find one at the head of the square!' He acknowledged her suggestion with a slight wave of his hand and began to walk away. She caught sight of his face briefly. Did I see tears, she wondered. Arthur in tears?

She lowered the window and slowly crossed to her desk. Arthur in tears? She sat at the desk and stared at a framed photograph of a young Marjorie Denning seated in a straight-back chair wearing a brocaded gown and immaculately coiffured. At her side stood a six year old boy in a velvet suit with pearl buttons, tightly clutching a toy sailboat, with what she now realised was an incredibly sad expression on his face.

What was that dreadful noise? Why it was *me*. It was a *sob*. Oh Arthur, were you so unhappy then too? She abruptly reached out and moved the photograph face downward on the desk. It was too late to make amends for Arthur. There was no point in berating herself for having been an inadequate mother. Years ago she had promised herself, no regrets, and she never broke a promise.

Now then, where was I? Oh, yes . . . Put a stop to what?

Laura has been attacked by a prowler resulting in a complete loss of memory. She performed a rapid mental autopsy and then murmured, 'Rubbish.' There's got to be more to it than that. Detective-Inspector Clive Fuller. Now why is that name familiar? Think. Think. Of course! He's written a book I've read. Arthur published it and sent me a copy. He's no ordinary investigating officer. Then Laura's is no ordinary case. Fuller has cracked a large number of major murder cases. Murder. *Murder?* 'Oh hell,' she said aloud.

Now why in the world would Laura want to kill anyone except perhaps Arthur and he's just left the house in tears, not in a coffin. Could Laura be driven to murder? I suppose anybody could be driven to murder when hatred is the chauffeur.

If the celebrated Laura Denning has committed murder, how was it kept from the newspapers? Harborford is a tiny village with a large mouth. No matter how much security you wrap around a crime, there's always a leak. She ran everything Arthur had told her through her mind again, from Laura's frantic phone call to him through her convalescence at Doctor Flint's sanatorium. Something was missing. He said he'd found Laura in a terrible state and brought her back to London. *What* terrible state? Laura had seemed perfectly relaxed and charming when she'd last visited her at Royalties the previous April, a spur-of-the-moment trip from nearby Wardsley where she'd been lecturing.

There'd been little discussion of the estrangement because it was unnecessary between women who understood each other as well as they did. The small cocktail party Laura had given for her that evening had been surprisingly pleasant, and so had been most of the guests. Was she nursing a secret desire *then* to do one of them in? Impossible. She was the life of her own party. It was the Laura she'd adored and admired as a bride. There wasn't a man in the room who didn't appear to be in love with her.

*Aha!*

Perhaps a crime of passion has been committed. Now who among those guests looked particularly passionate? There was the Doctor, and the sea captain, and the eminent Frank Welbeck and of course his hawk of a sister. Now who else? She worried her memory further and it soon complied. There was that dear little vicar who reminded her of a seraph in Harrods' window at Christmas, and she chuckled at the memory of him. Oh yes. The aunt and niece whom she'd referred to afterwards as the witch and sleeping beauty. Well if one of *them* was dead, we certainly would have heard about it.

Oh dear. Perhaps there really was a prowler and Laura killed him in self-defence and scrub it right now because there'd be no need for Fuller to return to Harborford with her. We'd have had the headlines weeks ago, Laura would have been exonerated and life would continue in its measured pace.

Now what's this silly tune I'm humming?

Probably from that dreadful musical comedy I had to endure last night. I dozed through most of it anyway. The very idea of a musical version of *A Doll's House. Goodbye, Nora* indeed!

I remember. Slowly she arose from the chair and, arms folded and deep in thought, she crossed to the window. It was towards the end of the party. Laura had whispered something to me about a storm brewing, but she wasn't referring to the weather. She meant two of her guests. It was one of those two I heard humming the tune, I remember that because it was beginning to get on my nerves and I think I said as much. I probably did because I usually do.

How important is all this? she asked herself. How can I offer crumbs when I'm ignorant of the nature of the crime? Hell and damnation! Small crumbs have led to the destruction of governments. April was two months ago, just a few weeks before Laura's misfortune.

She came to a decision and hurried to her telephone.

Laura and Fuller shared a bench in a secluded corner of the private park adjoining the sanatorium. Her notebook was open in her lap but her attention was focused on some honeysuckle where a bee was making an absolute pig of himself. Fuller had planned on Sunday to himself, but Laura's urgent message left at Scotland Yard that morning had found its way to him and he to Laura. She'd greeted him as though he'd been absent for months on an Arctic expedition though he'd visited her the previous day, and then she suggested the garden as the safest place from interruptions.

'I'd like to hear the dream,' he said gently.

'Nightmare,' she corrected him, abandoning bee and honeysuckle. She glanced down at the notebook and said, 'I hope you can make some sense out of this. I've been over it a dozen times this morning and all it does is continue to scare the daylights out of me. Amusingly enough, this nightmare's like a motion picture. It had background music throughout. That tune I keep humming.'

'Good.'

'Yes I thought you'd like that.' She referred to the notebook. 'At the beginning of the dream, the tune is very eerie as though it's being played in an echo chamber.'

'Fully orchestrated?'

'No, piano. Somebody picking out the notes with one finger.'

'There's a piano in your cottage.'

'I was afraid of that. But I'm outdoors when the dream begins. It's night, pitch black night. No moon, no stars, but I seem to know my way.' Fuller nodded encouragement. 'I think it's somewhere in the vicinity of the cottage because I can hear the roar of the surf and waves breaking.' Fuller was envisaging *Wuthering Heights* but said nothing. 'I realise there's someone walking behind me, but I'm not frightened because they're *humming* the tune.'

'Did you look behind?'

'No, I don't think so. I think I knew the person. Anyway, at this point I stumbled because the person caught my arm and kept me from going over.'

'Going over what?'

'The *cliff*. In fact, I think that was my first feeling of fright, but I'm not sure whether it's because I almost went over the cliff or whether there was some confusion as to the person attempting to *push* me.' Fuller gestured for her to continue. 'At this point the background music develops. It's becoming a full piano solo and quite professional.'

'You play very badly.'

'Arthur's told you, I suppose.' He smiled, and she thought with irony, Good Old Arthur. 'Well anyway, at this point I see a house and I start running towards it. There's a single light from it to guide me. The person behind is in full pursuit and I say pursuit because in the nightmare I really felt now as though I was being chased. Now I'm in the house.'

'Royalties?'

'I'm not sure. I don't think so. It's one huge room or at least one huge room in this house, ballroom size.'

'No ballrooms in your cottage.'

'I should think not. Anyway, in the centre of this room is some sort of tall column and I think it was white and here's where the violins joined in.'

'Very romantic.'

'Romantic hell, they were terribly scratchy and off-key, like a chorus of harpies and I got the feeling about this time that I was in some sort of house of worship. You know, as though this white column was some sort of replica of a native God, a form of totem.'

'Did the person following you come into the room?'

'Oh she was with me all the time.'

'*She?*'

'Oh yes, I'm positive it was a woman.'

'Why?'

'Because she was crying.'

'Men cry too.'

'Not the way *she* was crying. She was crying the *tune*. That's when the scratchy violins came in. By the way, I must tell you this entire nightmare now becomes one of those distorting mirrors you see in amusement parks. Everything's becoming out of shape, there's no proportion and I'm terribly frightened because the white column suddenly is holding a *knife*!'

'What sort of knife?'

'Well I've been assuming it's the carving knife.'

'What happens next?'

'The brass joins in.' Fuller was reaching for his pipe. 'Briefly, the scratchy violins subside, but then when the brass subsides, the volume of the scratchy violins is turned up again and this continues for a while in waves.'

'Like an argument?'

'Yes! That could very well be!' He was now holding a lighted match but abruptly blew the flame out, discarded the burnt match and placed the pipe back in his pocket. She glanced at the notebook and then continued. 'Oh, yes. Now comes the dialogue.' His eyebrows arched. 'Someone, I think it's a woman, says "Oh baby ... oh baby, baby."' She laughed nervously. 'Even nightmares can get a little silly sometimes, can't they?'

'Sometimes.'

'I'm glad you agree. Now comes the worst part. Drums.' He didn't react. 'Beating beating beating ... an incessant throb and causing me great pain. . . .'

'Like a heart-beat?'

'*Yes!* That must be it. Probably my heart pounding with fear! Because now I'm running around the room being pursued by the white column with the knife raised attempting to strike! Then I heard a scream, a terrible agonising scream and I think at first it's myself but it isn't ... and then ... then ...' He thought she'd paused to grab at her throat dramatically but instead she slapped a fly from her neck. '. . . Then it began to rain.'

'Outside?'

'No, *no . . . inside . . .* in the room . . . drenching me . . . the rain was *red . . . blood red!* And I hear laughter, sinister, frightening laughter and I rush to the door . . . but something . . . someone . . . I'm not sure about this . . . is barring my way . . . and I start screaming "Help! Help!" and I woke up screaming "help." '

He leaned forward. 'I want you to think hard. If your nightmare represents what I think it does, I want you to listen very carefully, and think *hard* before you answer. In the nightmare, before you started screaming for help, are you *sure* it wasn't that someone was barring your escape but because you were *too frozen with fear to move*?'

'Oh!' she gasped.

'I said *think*.' She thought while he tapped the pipe bowl on the back of the fence, after which he unscrewed the stem and poked at it with the cleaner he magically produced from his inside jacket pocket.

'Oh, I know what you're getting at,' she said with a groan, 'but I'm just not sure. Look . . . if I was frozen with fear . . . how could I have shouted for help?'

'Perhaps it wasn't you who did the shouting.'

Her author's blood began to boil as she spoke with an edge to her voice. 'Really, Mr Fuller, this is *my* nightmare and I don't think it requires much revision.' She waved the notebook under his nose. 'I've written it down exactly as I remembered it!'

'I think it's already been proven to you,' he said with the patience usually attributed to saints, 'that memory isn't completely reliable. You awaken from a nightmare. I assume you're frightened. The room is dark. You grope for the night light. You find it. You scramble for notebook and pencil. You're still a bit hazy. You begin to scribble. Didn't you at some point, after all this activity, have to pause and prod your memory?'

'I suppose so.'

'Don't get peevish. I'm only trying to help. You realise of course you dreamt the murder.'

'Of course I do!'

'Then it's quite possible that in your nightmare you were frozen with fear!'

'If you insist,' she shouted angrily, 'then I was frozen with fear! Far be it from me to ruin your day! But it was my god-damn nightmare and I don't recall being frozen with fear. I was shouting help and that's what woke me up and I own the copyright!'

'Beautiful.'

She began to flush with embarrassment until she realised he hadn't been looking at her when he spoke, but at a butterfly gliding around a rose bush. 'Yes isn't it,' she said. 'I think that species is called *Vanessa* ... you know, like in Redgrave.'

He turned to look at her. 'How do you know that?'

She replied swiftly and with an air of hauteur. 'Because Fiona ...'

'Because Fiona *what*?' he said swiftly.

'Because Fiona ...' she began again, and then made a gesture of defeat. 'That's it, there isn't any more.'

'It's encouraging though, isn't it?'

'Yes,' she agreed with alacrity, 'yes it is! Oh indeed it is!' She flung her arms around him and then just as abruptly pulled away saying, 'Oh, sorry.'

'Quite all right.'

'Isn't it marvellous the way Fiona popped out of my mouth like that!'

'I suspect there'll be more of the same from now on.'

'Fiona.' She repeated the name as though it was being assessed. *Maybe it's the moon over Cornwall*.... Her hand flew to her mouth and her eyes linked with Fuller's. Slowly, her hand lowered as she spoke. 'It's *her* song. It must be. *It must be*.' She was trembling. 'Clive ... I have a picture of a woman in my mind.' She sounded like a vaudeville mind reader's assistant announcing she has a woman in the balcony.

'Describe her.'

'My height . . . closely cropped chestnut hair . . . hazel eyes . . . lovely skin . . . very lovely skin . . . the face itself isn't conventionally beautiful . . . it has some sort of quality all it's own . . . funny . . . I think of the word "noble" . . . it's not a happy face I'm seeing, Clive . . . but I think it's Fiona. Is it?'

'It could fit the other woman in the photograph I saw in Auriol Kendall's house. Remember I've never met Fiona. She was away on a field trip.' He wondered if she'd returned. He wanted desperately to meet and talk to Fiona Cooper. 'But closely cropped hair fits the bill.'

'It doesn't tally with any other woman you've met in Harborford, does it?'

He thought for a few moments and then said, 'No, not one bit.'

'Then it's Fiona, and she looks very unhappy, just the way she looked in my nightmare. . . . *Oh!*'

'Congratulations.'

'*Oh!*'

'I knew you didn't remember it all. One rarely does.'

'I think it was Fiona who was walking *behind* me!'

'Or pursuing you.'

'Whatever, I think it was Fiona. I can't wait to see her!' He privately shared that with her. 'Clive?'

'Yes?'

'If she was with me in the nightmare, and you think I was dreaming the murder, then Fiona . . .' Her voice trailed away, like the conversation of a passer by. There was no need for him to say anything, he knew what she was thinking. Fiona might have been a witness to the murder which could explain her sudden decision to leave Harborford. He wanted desperately to get back to the Yard, contact the village and check out if Fiona had returned, and just as quickly a second sense told him she probably hadn't, but

98

still checking might not go unrewarded. Tomorrow he'd be in Harborford with a fresh scent to guide him. But could it wait until tomorrow? If Fiona had bravely decided to return home and could identify the murderer, then she was in danger. But on the other hand, he reminded himself, if the murderer was Laura ...

'What a terrible expression on your face,' he heard Laura comment.

He mustered a jocular tone. 'I have a variety of those.'

'*There you are!*'

They both stared in the direction of the sudden intrusion. They saw a handsome woman in her mid-sixties, smartly dressed in a well-tailored tweed suit with matching tam o'shanter crowning her head, her right hand waving a large alligator bag and a lavish smile stretching across her face. Clive Fuller recognised her immediately. Laura had to think for a moment. She'd seen the face before. Newspapers. Television. She groped frantically in her mind as the woman trudged the path that led to their corner.

Of course, thought Laura, swiftly returning the woman's smile, it's my mother-in-law!


Chapter Nine

Fuller was already standing when Laura arose to embrace Dame Marjorie and then introduced Fuller. 'It's just my face you recognise, isn't it?' Dame Marjorie asked Laura knowledgeably.

'I'm afraid that's it,' said Laura as Dame Marjorie settled herself on the bench, pulling Laura next to her, 'but I have a feeling we like each other immensely.'

'Oh indeed!' said the older woman warmly as Fuller settled on the grass at their feet, 'otherwise, I wouldn't be here.' She looked at Fuller. 'I had the devil's own time tracking you down. Luckily for me Laura'd left a message for you at the Yard this morning.' She told them of Arthur's visit earlier that day and their conversation, emphasising his somewhat mysterious allusions to a possible *cause celebre*. She then imperiously demanded the full story of the Laura incident (as she put it). Fuller hesitated and the determined woman prodded him with a threat to get her facts from his superior. Fuller told her everything. During his recital, Dame Marjorie frequently patted Laura's hand sympathetically and interjected the occasional 'How awful, how beastly, dreadful' and 'Oh you poor darling', meaning Laura, not Fuller. At one point she fixed her *pince-nez* to the bridge of her nose to examine Laura's left cheek and was satisfied there was no longer a trace of the three scratches.

When Fuller finished speaking, Dame Marjorie launched eagerly into the April weekend she'd spent with Laura and the cocktail party. A past mistress at oratory, she held them intrigued and spellbound. At the conclusion she said, waving the *pince-nez* like a baton, 'Now, mind you, I have no idea if this argument has any bearing on the dreadful event that followed, but I had the feeling, Mr Fuller, you need all the ammunition you can get, so here I am.'

Fuller expressed his gratitude and then asked her, 'Do you recall which of the women were arguing?'

'Did I say it was two women?' Her look of astonishment was the one she usually reserved for her West End butcher when he quoted the price of beef. 'It wasn't two women. It wasn't two women at all!' She paused provocatively and Fuller complimented her to himself for mastering the art of creating an effect. 'It was a *man* and a woman!' Laura was thinking Dame Marjorie should try her hand at writing thrillers with her innate talent for sustaining suspense. 'The man was Frank Welbeck.' Laura and Fuller exchanged glances as Dame Marjorie declared a silent intermission by rummaging in her purse, finding a dainty handkerchief and delicately blowing her nose. After a punctuating sniffle she

100

resumed speaking. 'The woman's name escapes me. However, she was continually humming some rather saccharine melody.'

Laura hummed.

'That's it!' exclaimed Dame Marjorie, 'that's the tune. She was driving me mad with it. I believe you told me,' pointing the *pince-nez* at Laura, 'she was some sort of bacteriologist.'

'Lepidopterist.'

'Ah yes! Of course! I recall suggesting she try humming *Poor Butterfly* and she said she knew very little about opera and since *Poor Butterfly* had nothing to do with opera I let the matter drop. I remember diverting the conversation to the strange scent she was wearing. . . .'

'Heliotrope?' interjected Fuller.

Dame Marjorie's eyes widened. 'I think you're right, I think it *was* heliotrope. Yes! Yes! It's coming back to me. She said it was a perfume she couldn't normally afford, a gift from an admirer or something like that. Then she interrupted to snap something at her friend about drinking too much. . . .'

'Her aunt?' suggested Fuller.

'No, no . . . *Welbeck* . . . that's when they went outdoors and you, Laura, whispered something to me about a storm brewing meaning Welbeck and the butterfly creature.'

'Fiona Cooper,' said Laura.

Dame Marjorie stared at the sky as she ran the name through her head, finally giving it official clearance and agreeing it was Fiona Cooper.

'Did you overhear any of the argument?' Fuller asked.

'I'm afraid not,' replied Dame Marjorie, 'they were outside and I was in. But the hawk did.'

'The hawk?' This was a new one on Laura.

'Welbeck's sister. Well she looks like a hawk, doesn't she?'

Fuller came to Laura's rescue. 'It's a fairly accurate description.'

'How nice you agree. She was standing at the open window with that dear little Vicar person, but paying absolutely no attention to anything he said. I could see her straining to catch the intercourse going on outside. Then Laura went out and brought Fiona back into the house and Welbeck went stalking off towards the cliffs. After your guests had departed, Laura, I seem to recall asking you what the hullaballoo was all about, but you pleaded ignorance. You were lying of course, but I let the matter drop.'

Laura turned to Fuller. 'It must have been Fiona who spent the night in the guest bedroom.'

'The heliotrope seems to point to it.'

'And she was in my nightmare.'

Dame Marjorie hadn't looked so rattled since the day she was first introduced to Bernadette Devlin. Fuller explained Laura's nightmare to which Dame Marjorie commented with delight, 'How like Cocteau!' Then she shuddered. 'Bloody knives, bloody kitchens, a missing corpse, amnesia ... my poor dear Laura, it's as gruesome as the thought of your reconciling with Arthur. You're not, are you?'

Laura spoke firmly and without hesitation. 'Sorry, no.'

Dame Marjorie patted her hand again. 'It's for the best, you know. You were a changed girl when I visited you at Royalties. That old vivacity I'd missed so much was back. There wasn't a man at that party that wasn't devouring you with his eyes, especially that rogue Welbeck. I don't suppose you can remember if he ever finished that statue of Charlotte Bronte?'

'Charlotte Corday,' said Laura with a laugh.

'I'm so bad on names.' She addressed Fuller. 'Welbeck did me the rare honour of a peek at his work in progress the morning of the party. A subtle bit of politics on his part, I'm quite sure.' She favoured Fuller with a wicked wink. 'I can be quite influential in assisting with grants. I didn't like the work one bit, though of course I refrained from telling him that. Corday ... Corday ... of course, she stabbed Marat. Now isn't *that* interesting, Mr Fuller?'

'In what way?' he inquired politely.

'Don't be so dense. Laura poses for the statue of a woman whose weapon was a knife, and then Laura is discovered with a similar weapon in her hand? Surely *that's* an interesting coincidence!'

Fuller flicked an ant from his trouser turn-up. 'Yes, Dame Marjorie, a very interesting coincidence. How clever of you to notice.'

'I don't miss much,' and she nudged Laura gently.

Laura said quickly, 'You certainly don't.' Then for want of anything better, 'How was Arthur?'

Dame Marjorie shook her head sadly. 'Not very happy, I'm afraid. He should have had a different mother.' Her bag was open again and she extracted a pair of gloves, and then she caught Fuller's eye. 'You are censuring me, Mr Fuller.' She shrugged. 'I told that to Arthur years ago, and it was the first time in our lives we've ever been in agreement. The second was when he married Laura. Now I must go. I have a luncheon engagement.' She wriggled her fingers in the gloves and then got to her feet. Fuller arose from the grass with agility, brushing his trousers as Laura stood and faced her mother-in-law.

'Thank you for coming,' said Laura, taking Dame Marjorie's hand.

'I would have come sooner had I known.' They embraced. 'It'll all come out right. I know it will. If I may, I'll be in touch with you at Royalties. I'll be aching to hear about the fresh developments. Goodbye, Mr Fuller. I hope my small contribution has been of some help.'

He said as he shook her hand, 'It's been a tremendous help.'

'Well!' she said with a snort, 'I'm sure this case will be in your next book. Remember to give credit where credit is due and for God's sake don't spell Marjorie with a *g*.'

She turned for one last look at Laura, impulsively moved forward and kissed her cheek, then rapidly strode away.

Fuller suggested a stroll and they took a path that bordered the iron fence protecting the park.

'A penny for them,' said Fuller.

'I was thinking of Fiona and Frank Welbeck. That's obviously as new to you as it is to me or you'd have mentioned it before.' She looked at him sharply. 'You would have, wouldn't you?'

'I've told you everything I know. It's not the sort of thing either Auriol Kendall or Emaline Welbeck would have revealed anyway. They each have someone to protect. On the other hand, my investigation in Harborford was mostly concerned with you and your relationships. There was no reason for me then to go off at tangents. Looking back on it now, I realise just about every answer I got from anyone was a guarded statement.

'Starting tomorrow, there'll be a new approach. I've laid the groundwork. I'm familiar with the people in Harborford. You've been making wonderful progress. I think the nightmare is terribly significant.' He was counting off with his fingers. 'We know now heliotrope and the tune are associated with Fiona. There's some sort of relationship between Fiona and Welbeck or why would his possessive sister strain so hard to eavesdrop? It's a probability Fiona spent the night or part of that night at your cottage, and *then* went off on this so-called field trip. If we can trust Dame Marjorie's memory, then Fiona's heliotrope scent was a gift ... from someone in the village or *elsewhere*? Auriol Kendall admits to an argument that might have triggered Fiona's sudden departure, or had it already been *planned*?

'Then there's your mother-in-law's shrewd observation. You're posing for Charlotte Corday and later found with a blood-stained knife in your hand. If you didn't actually commit the murder yourself, then it was the work of a very warped, vengeful person. Yet,' he said with a sigh, 'everyone I've interviewed expressed nothing but the deepest affection for you.'

104

Muttered Laura, 'Somebody believes you can kill with kindness.'

'That white column in your nightmare. I don't recall seeing anything like it in the houses I visited in the village. White column.' He massaged his chin. 'Flagpole? Monument? Statue?' He grabbed her hand.

'What?'

'Statue! Ballroom! What's the size of Welbeck's studio?'

'Big.' She felt a trickle of nervous perspiration making its way down her spine. She was able to say *big*. 'Did you hear what I said? I said "big" without having to prod my mind. It came out. Just like *that*,' snapping her fingers.

'The studio is a converted barn, and that's big. It's just possible you and Fiona visited the studio that Sunday night.' He rubbed his hands together with excitement.

'Welbeck didn't mention it when you questioned him.'

'Everyone in your charmed little circle seems to be guilty of the sin of omission. A person could get indigestion from too much red herring and I'm not all that much of a fish fancier.' Laura made a mental note, easy on the fish with Fuller.

'How do I behave tomorrow?'

'About what?'

'With the friends I won't recognise!'

'I've given you complete descriptions of them. They'll match.'

'That isn't what I mean. What attitude do I take? The cock and bull about a prowler and the attack! My amnesia!'

'Just be your old vivacious self.' She realised his strange cackle was a bad imitation of Dame Marjorie.

'The men,' she said in despair, 'what do I do about *them*?'

'Do whatever comes naturally,' he said whimsically. 'Stop worrying about it. I'll be with you every possible moment and announce them under my breath as each

105

appears. Nurse Murdock knows you're to be packed and ready by nine in the morning.'

'What time's the train?'

'Our helicopter leaves at ten.'

'Helicopter!' She flung her arms out and did a quick pirouette. 'What an entrance!'

'*Din-Dins!*'

Nurse Murdock was waving from a second storey window. Laura froze, shuddered, and then found a smile for Fuller. 'Dear Nurse Murdock. She's such a treasure. Must we put up with her in Harborford?'

'Yes,' he said solemnly. 'You might just as well know. She's one of our best policewomen.'

Laura's shoulders sagged. 'That had never occurred to me.'

'That giddy exterior of hers is quite deceptive.' She was following Fuller towards the main building, and he was speaking to her over his shoulder. His head was in a direct line with the sun, and his profile looked to Laura like the head of a Roman emperor embossed on a coin. 'We met five years ago when she saw me through a bad attack of pneumonia. In a way I suppose I guided her decision to go into police work. She's devoted to me.'

*She's devoted to me.* Din-dins be damned. Laura had lost her appetite.

'By the way, she came up with a suggestion the other day that made me feel like a hopeless fool for not having thought of it myself.'

'What was that?' asked Laura unenthusiastically.

'She wondered if I'd checked the cutlery in your kitchen to see if the murder weapon was part of a set. Murdock has the feeling that yours is the sort of house in which things match.' Laura quickened her pace and caught up with him. 'Of course people do buy the odd carving knife, but when it is pearl-handled, one assumes that sort of thing is part of a set. If not part of your set,' he added casually, 'then perhaps part of another household's.'

106

'But would the assailant have been stupid enough to leave behind a weapon that can be traced?'

'Perhaps not stupid enough, but hysterical enough. We have to look for slips like that. Sometimes they're the only break we get. If you've nothing more urgent to think about this afternoon, try concentrating on pearl-handled knives. I might add, expensive pearl-handled knives of a sort common at the turn of the last century.' He rubbed the tip of his nose. 'They were popular wedding gifts.'

'I suppose you've questioned Arthur about *our* wedding gifts.'

'He was a bit hazy about it. After all, eight years is quite a long time. But he seemed fairly positive there were no carving knives. Of course he couldn't account for what you might have purchased for the cottage after your estrangement.'

'Good old Arthur.' They reached the entrance to the building.

'Don't underestimate Arthur too much. Just because something's dull doesn't mean it can't be blunt. Have a nice lunch. See you in the morning.'

On that cryptic note he left her standing in the doorway with her arms tightly interlocked, lips exaggeratedly clamped together to stifle an angry comment on the mateyness of British men. She took a deep breath and entered the building, taking the stairs to the second storey two at a time. On the first storey landing a new thought caused her to grip the bannister.

Murdock. Policewoman. *Notebook*. She's had many opportunities to read the notebook. Everything, including the intimate details. Oh, Murdock, if you have and spilled the beans about my feelings towards Fuller . . .

She realised she was clenching and unclenching her fists.

Arthur Denning knew his mother must have seen his tears and didn't give a damn. He hadn't found a taxi at the top of the square because he didn't want one. He had

107

paused outside his mother's house because he had no idea what to do with himself for the rest of the day. He had nowhere to go, no one to visit, no one to have lunch or supper with, and couldn't think of anyone who might welcome his company. The tears that welled up were not of self-pity but frustration and self-rage. When his mother had called to him from the window, he resisted an angry urge to tell her to stuff herself, not knowing that if he had, it might have gained him a modicum of respect from that indomitable person.

She had advanced him the money to start his publishing business, an investment returned many times over, but the only delight she seemed to take in its success was being on its free mailing list. When he realised winning her love was as hopeless as telling her to keep an opinion to herself, he bought an airedale. He still bore a scar on his right thigh where it bit him. Then he met Laura and all seemed right with the world. But he had no green thumb for relationships. Laura had done her best to be the wife she thought he wanted; dull, colourless and withdrawn. He did nothing to stop the bloom from fading. He didn't know how. When she began to revive in Harborford she started a vigorous spring cleaning and swept him out the door. He didn't resist. He didn't know how.

'*Have you been having an affair?*'

'*What difference does that make? After all, Mother, I'm only human.*'

Had Dame Marjorie noticed the difficulty he had speaking those words? How *only human* almost stuck in his throat and caused him to choke?

He was now sitting on a bench overlooking the Thames across from Royal Festival Hall. His bowler hat was at his side brim upward, and from the dolorous expression he now imagined on his face, it wouldn't have surprised him if passersby dropped coins in the hat.

His thoughts returned to Laura and the unerasable memory of the blood-stained knife in her hand. The knife,

108

the awful incriminating knife. Why hadn't he used his head *then*? Why didn't I do something about it *then*? *Why don't I do something about it now?*

Because it's too late. It's gone too far. For the first time in my life, something has gone *too far*. 'Heaven help me,' he whispered to himself.

There might still be a miracle reserved for me.


Laura sat at the table near the window staring glumly at the tray of food. 'I can't eat this,' she said to Nurse Murdock.

'I can get you something else,' said Nurse Murdock with concern.

'It isn't a matter of substitutions. I simply haven't any appetite.' She pushed the tray away. 'Please sit down,' she said, indicating the chair opposite. Nurse Murdock obeyed and waited while Laura lit a cigarette.

'Excited about tomorrow?' she asked enthusiastically as Laura realised this was the first time she seriously examined the young woman's appearance. What she saw was a scrubbed face with apple cheeks, alert blue eyes and the overall antiseptic good looks that might just suit Clive Fuller's taste.

'Mr Fuller's told me you're a policewoman.'

'Oh *that*,' said Nurse Murdock airily. 'I thought you'd cottoned on to that *days* ago. You're so *clever*.'

Laura ignored what was undoubtedly a genuine compliment and pressed on. 'You've read my notebook, I suppose.'

'Only in the line of duty,' said Nurse Murdock hastily.

'Then Fuller also knows the contents.'

Nurse Murdock smiled. 'He knows only what I think pertinent to the case. I've completely respected your private thoughts about him.'

'Thank you,' said Laura with difficulty. 'You realise it would have embarrassed me terribly.' She found the strength to muster a nervous smile. 'I suppose there's a bit of the schoolgirl in all of us.'

'I understand completely how you feel about him.' She moved her chair closer. 'I felt the same way when I first met him.' My God, thought Laura, girl talk! 'I suppose he's told you about that first meeting.' Laura nodded. 'It was sheer infatuation that made me follow him into police work. My friends at St Mary's thought I was crazy, but . . .' and she sighed deeply and clucked her tongue like castanets, 'there's no explaining when the heart has its reasons, is there?'

'Oh, there certainly isn't,' agreed Laura, privately wondering which women's magazine Nurse Murdock read. 'Did Mr Fuller suspect your feelings?'

'Oh, heavens yes. There's nothing subtle about *me*!' She flipped a wrist laughing heartily and Laura was beginning to like her. 'But then I met Brian and all came right with the world.'

Brian. Laura heard a tinkle in her brain and then quickly it struck home. 'Cummings? *Our* Brian Cummings?'

'Mine,' said Nurse Murdock contentedly. 'We've been married three years now. As soon as we've saved enough money and he can take a leave of absence, he's having his adenoids removed.' She was staring out the window. 'I hope he's all right.' Laura waited. 'He's such a poor sailor.'

'Where is he?'

Nurse Murdock turned to Laura with a look of surprise. 'Hasn't Clive told you? He's in Harborford with four of our men!'

The security, Laura realised. 'Perhaps I wasn't supposed to know.'

'I don't see why not. Clive tells you everything. He has tremendous respect for you.' Laura resisted an urge to sing. 'They've gone down as a fishing party. They're staying at the Inn. They've been there since yesterday. Poor Brian. I packed his seasick pills. I hope he remembers to take them.'

Laura was glad there was no reason for her to stand up. Her feet felt weak and flaccid. The enormity of the return

110

to Harborford the next day had started to overwhelm her. Security. Five men, and for their cover, a fishing party. She found her voice. 'Mr Fuller expects trouble, doesn't he?'

'Let me put it this way. The security is a necessary precaution. The two Harborford constables haven't been very successful ... uh. ...'

Laura came to her assistance. 'Finding the missing body.'

'Well yes.' Nurse Murdock nervously tugged at her hem.

'So when not fishing, the men will be out exploring.'

'Yes.'

Laura sat back in the chair and examined the lit end of her cigarette. 'Nurse Murdock...'

'Elaine,' Nurse Murdock interjected cosily.

'Thank you. Elaine, you said Clive tells me everything. That was very sweet of you, but I don't think he has.'

'Oh?' It was spoken with complete innocence.

'I've been questioning to myself some statements he made about his investigation in the village.'

'Oh, really?' Laura privately hoped Nurse Murdock had been told where babies come from, then realised the naivete was a practised, self-protective pose. Clive Fuller wouldn't be working with a nincompoop. Laura decided a no-nonsense attitude could be advantageous and said:

'Any help you can give me will be more than appreciated.'

'I'll do my best.'

Laura crossed her legs. 'The day I awoke from the coma, Clive said something to the effect that none of my friends in Harborford seemed to know Arthur and I were separated. In the light of subsequent information about the life I've possibly been leading down there, it seems a bit ridiculous.'

Nurse Murdock said with relief, 'Oh that's an easy one. He and I have sifted through that one at great length. We think the obvious one is this, you were working on a new book and everyone knows when you do you're hell on wheels and to the innocent it was simply a matter of Arthur

111

staying out of your way until it was safe to return. But,' she said softly, 'we think that's mostly where your women friends are concerned. One of the men, if not all of them, must have known you were definitely estranged. We think you protected yourself there by denying any thought of divorce. You must also understand the spur of the moment prowler story had Clive a bit boxed in with his questioning. To delve too deeply into your relationships with Mr Denning might have made the smarter ones question the validity of the fabrication. That's why he's insisted Mr Denning return with us tomorrow.' She pursed her lips and shook her head sadly. 'Clive wasn't at all happy with his investigation. Not one bit. You know how people are in those villages. Among themselves, they gossip away freely. But with strangers, they become tight-lipped and guarded. They protect their own.' Her voice brightened. 'And they consider you one of their own.'

'That's very comforting,' commented Laura drily.

'Anything else?'

'Yes.' Nurse Murdock had the alert look of a sentry on guard duty. 'That Monday morning, was my phone working?'

'I suppose there's no sidestepping this one,' said Nurse Murdock in defeat after a thirty-second pause. 'No. Your phone was not working. Clive will probably have my scalp for this.'

'Serves him right for spilling the beans about you being a policewoman. He must have known when he did I'd start chipping away at you. Why wasn't it working?'

'It had been torn from the kitchen wall.'

'I see. That's hardly something *I* would have done, is it.'

'Well, that's what I think.'

'Clive doesn't?'

'I don't think he's sure.'

'Why not?'

'Oh dear ... oh the hell with it ... if you were in some

112

sort of rage, you just might have.'

'Quite logical. Now let's take it a step further, as I'm sure Clive already has but for reasons of his own has preferred I be kept in the dark. Arthur arrives, finds me in the kitchen, carries me to the sitting room, places me on the couch, and let us assume now finds the phone is not working. I'm presuming there's an extension in the sitting room.'

'And in your bedroom.'

'Fine. So in order to get Dr Kettering, Arthur has to drive to the village for him, right?'

'Yes.'

'My nearest neighbours are the Welbecks?'

'Yes.'

'But Arthur didn't rush to the Welbecks?'

'No.'

'He drove to the village.'

'Yes.'

'What was Arthur's explanation for *that one*?'

'He said he was in a panic and not thinking straight.'

'All right, having come to know Arthur a bit better, I just might accept that for the moment.' She folded her arms after stubbing out the cigarette. 'Then I was quite alone on that couch for about ... oh ... half an hour or so?'

'About that.' Nurse Murdock looked puzzled. 'What about it? You were in a cataleptic state then.'

'I know I know. But Arthur makes no attempt to revive me or release the knife from my hand.'

'He couldn't.'

'Did he try?'

'He said he didn't. Panic, you know.'

'Of course. Panic.' She diverted her attention to the tray of food.

'There's that song again! You're humming!'

'What ...?' *There's that song again.* 'Oh dear,' she said swiftly, 'I feel so tired. I think I could use a nap.'

'You could also use some food!'

113

'I couldn't eat a bite.' She leaned forward and took Elaine's hand. 'Thank you, Elaine. Thank you for being so cooperative.'

'Oh well,' said Nurse Murdock as she arose from the chair and lifted the tray, 'you would have got it out of Clive sooner or later. You have your nap. I'll look in on you with a snack in a few hours.'

'None of that anchovy paste!' cried Laura as Nurse Murdock shut the door behind her. She left the chair and went to the window and leaned her head against the pane to cool her brow. She closed her eyes and in her mind two words began rapidly flashing on and off like distress signals.

*Arthur hates Arthur hates Arthur hates Arthur hates . . .*

Chapter Ten

After he left Laura at the entrance to the sanatorium, Clive Fuller found a phone kiosk. He looked up the number he wanted in his private directory, found a new coin for the coin box, silently prayed Doctor Emmanuel Herkimer would be at home and dialled. His prayer was answered and fifteen minutes later he sat over cups of coffee in the lounge of the Doctor's flat in Montagu Square. The Doctor, who had a long and honoured history of consultation with Scotland Yard, listened attentively as Fuller repeated Laura's nightmare. After Fuller patiently complied twice with the doctor's request to repeat the nightmare, Herkimer sat back in his chair, crossed a leg, vigorously scratched the calf, pulled up the sock, uncrossed his legs and asked Fuller if he'd like something to eat.

When Fuller politely declined, Herkimer crossed the other leg, repeated the process of calf and sock, uncrossed the leg and offered a brandy which Fuller also politely declined. The Doctor lowered his head to his chest, not in

114

rejection, but in thought. Fuller knew his ears weren't deceiving him when the doctor began to make squeaky noises. After a minute of discordant serenade, the doctor raised his head and kicked off his shoes. Fuller studied a hole in the doctor's left sock and decided Mrs Herkimer had not yet recovered from her most recent nervous breakdown.

Herkimer blew air out of his mouth, making his lips quiver. 'I am not a gypsy fortune teller.' Fuller was well aware of this and refrained from saying so. 'When the person is not a patient, analysing a dream can be a bit dodgy.' Fuller had expected this. 'It's a common type of nightmare. On a first hearing, it's rather sexual. The knife, the white column . . . castration . . . very obviously castration. But out of context, it is very difficult to be sure.' He repositioned himself in the chair. 'I don't want to mislead you. Tell me about the person who dreamt this, the facts of the case.'

Fuller did so. When he finished, the doctor unwound his feet, massaged them each in turn, and then with an effort slipped them back into the shoes. 'Laura Denning.' He spoke her name like a judge pronouncing sentence. 'Am . . . nes . . . i . . . ahhh!' He screwed up his face and scratched his chin. 'She doesn't strike me as the type, but then, I never thought the French would devalue the franc. I said it's a common type of nightmare and I'm not changing my opinion. Very common.' To Fuller he made it sound as though it was also beneath contempt. Herkimer pointed a chubby index finger at Fuller. '*You* of course think it's the solution to the murder. Well it isn't. But I'll tell you what I think it *might* signify.'

Fuller pulled at an earlobe and waited. The doctor was busy putting the pleat back in a trouser leg. When he had finished, he looked at Clive with a squint. 'I don't suppose I could get her on a couch for a couple of hours?' Fuller said he preferred not. 'You're probably right,' said the Doctor, 'she's obviously under enough stress as it is. Okay, I'll try to put it to you as simply as possible. There's castration

115

there all right, probably Mrs Denning's guilt about her husband. She is in this dream confusing her guilt with the actual crime.' Fuller leaned forward.

'This big room which you say could be the sculptor's studio. This is a very ordinary device of nightmares. It could also represent her *life*,' the arms were dramatically outstretched, 'and for her *life*, you could also read, her *home*. The white column you say might be this statue of Charlotte Corday for which she has been posing.' He began nodding his head vigorously. 'That's very good. A statue signifies creativity, also strength. It could represent Mrs Denning's *own* talents. It is possible she sees these threatened. Now that song ... could you hum it again please?' Fuller cleared his throat and hummed. 'Very romantic, very sexual ... not your humming, the melody itself.' Fuller hoped he'd hummed in tune. 'Your Mrs Denning appears to hunger for romance, but she is somewhat repressed. I think the rumours of her various affairs are a slight exaggeration, but she is privately revelling in the reputation.' The shoes were off again and he was rubbing his feet together. Fuller expected a spark to catch but none appeared.

'What about "oh baby, baby"?'

'She insists she did not speak those words herself?'

'Yes.'

'Possibly the woman she was with in the dream, the one who kept her from going off the cliff, the one she also confuses as a pursuer?'

'Possibly,' said Fuller with a shrug.

'Well ... there is definitely a connection here with the husband she feels she has castrated. I wish she could have clarified the person accompanying, pursuing ... whichever.' He thought for a moment. 'Does she perhaps have a nickname for a friend such as "baby"?'

'Not to my knowledge.'

'Is there someone in her immediate circle who is *pregnant*?'

'That hasn't come up either.'

116

'And in the nightmare, she hears a woman crying.' He looked perplexed and Fuller's heart sank. 'And the song is played first by one finger on a piano and then screeching violins, etcetera, etcetera.' He was making spirals with his right hand. 'That is also quite common. They are usually representative of human voices. The one-finger pianist, since you say there is a piano in her cottage, could be herself. The screeching violins could represent a discordant argument, between women most probably, they always screech like harpies. You've met my wife.'

'How is Marta?'

'Worse, bless her.' He left the chair and crossed to a bar and poured himself a brandy. He held up the bottle towards Fuller who shook his head. Cupping the brandy glass in both hands and gently swirling the liquid, he returned to his chair. 'The red rain,' he finally said. 'Freud, in case you didn't know, saw rain as symbolic of a sexual desire. When it is dreamt as red, the desire is usually interpreted as one of frustrating intensity. You of course have been seeing it as the blood spilled by the victim. Also possible.' He sipped the brandy, smacked his lips, said 'Ahhh!' and then sighed. 'I can't do much better than this, Clive, without knowing the patient's history from her own lips. I see you have been taking notes like the good investigator you are, so at your leisure you can try to make of it what you will. For example, her attempt to escape that room and her way being barred. *I* see it as her desperate desire to crash through the wall surrounding her memory, but what bars her egress is her own fear of revealing herself a murderess.

'Actually, Clive, if she did not commit this crime herself, I tend to believe she was definitely a witness to it. Prior to the time the crime occured, she undoubtedly had been suffering great personal stress over her private problems and *willed* herself into this cataleptic state. It's not unusual. I'm having the same situation with Marta right now. Marta unfortunately has gone one step further,' he stared into the brandy and Fuller thought his voice would break but it

117

didn't, 'and driven herself into total oblivion. Your Mrs Denning is obviously made of sterner stuff. The nightmare proves this ... her association of a butterfly with this friend...'

'Fiona Cooper.'

'Yes ... yes ... and also the song. The possibility this Cooper person spent the night at Mrs Denning's cottage ... the probability that in the nightmare it is also this woman who accompanies her and as you suggest was also a witness to the murder. You say she left the village presumably sometime that morning?'

'According to her aunt.'

'Do you know if she has returned?'

'I'm checking on that.'

'Yes. I think she will have a great deal to tell you ... if you find her.' Fuller didn't ask for an elaboration of the statement. He had his own theories about Fiona Cooper's actions and was not going to discuss them with Herkimer.

'Dr Flint thinks the return of Laura's memory might be a very slow process.'

'Oh ho, but I do disagree! I decidedly disagree! Look what you already have from her!' He was holding the glass outstretched as though it contained everything Laura had told Fuller to date. 'You return with her to the village to-morrow? She'll remember more ... and more, etcetera, etcetera...' he waved the same hand in spirals and ignored the brandy sloshing on to his trousers. 'It will all come back to her the more secure she begins to feel that she is innocent of this crime.' Herkimer winked. 'That's up to you, of course.' He downed the remaining brandy in one gulp and placed the glass on the floor. 'I can say no more, Clive. It would be unethical of me to make suppositions and in a sense, damaging to Mrs Denning. It's a lovely nightmare though. Common, but quite lovely.' He smacked his lips as though he had completely digested the nightmare and found it a culinary delight. 'She would be such an interesting patient. She does, of course, feel a tremendous affinity

118

with this sculptor, as both are creative, and creativity is obviously something Mrs Denning respects and would go to great lengths to protect. The husband of course is inartistic and therefore inferior, to Mrs Denning that is. Yes, yes, she will find the strength to face life again ... probably much sooner than you have dared hope.'

His head jerked forward with a serious expression on his face as he wagged the index finger and cautioned Fuller, 'But you must not tell her this in an attempt to force the process. You wish to break your case, of course, and the sooner the better, but with Mrs Denning forewarned would not be forearmed. The process might reverse itself and then of course you are lost. You have been handling her extremely well, but proceed with caution. When she sees this village again, the cottage, the people with whom she has been involved there ... the veil will slowly begin to lift.' He chuckled deep in his throat. 'And then of course, her life might not be worth a farthing.'

Clive Fuller owned a small house in a cul-de-sac in St John's Wood. He had walked home from Dr Herkimer's flat. He needed the time to think, to redigest and sift again the time he'd spent with Dr Herkimer. As he inserted the key in his lock, he could hear the phone ringing in the sitting room. He reached the phone in five long strides, and heard Elaine Murdock's voice on the other end.

She repeated the question and answer session with Laura over the uneaten lunch, Fuller smiling as she spoke with a mental picture of Laura extracting the answers she sought. He silently and happily reassured himself that the authoress was once more in command of her deductive powers and, after hanging up the phone, was almost convinced she would have a possible solution long before he did.

He dwelled again on Dr Herkimer's sketchy interpretation of the nightmare, then thought briefly of Marta Herkimer and said aloud, 'Physician heal thyself'. He reached for his private directory, consulted a page, found a number and dialled the Grace and Favour Inn in Harborford. His wristwatch told him it was ten minutes to five. He spoke into the phone and asked for Brian Cummings.

At about the time Clive Fuller was concluding his meeting with Dr Herkimer, the *Atlantis* was docking in its berth in Harborford. Eight hours earlier it had set its compass for the fishing bed some twenty miles offshore, gliding smoothly across a calm sea like a child's finger making an inroad on the icing of a freshly baked cake. At noon, the fishing party of five were in high spirits and Sean Coleridge was finding them an unusually amiable lot. Hansel and Gretel would have had little trouble following the ship's course thanks to the line of empty beer tins bobbing in its wake. Even the fish were unusually cooperative and there was a fine haul on board within two hours.

Brian Cummings, who always made it his duty to rehearse an assignment, had memorised a number of bawdy sea chanteys and, after swallowing two anti-seasick pills, serenaded the company until they were deaf to everything but the screeching of the gulls overhead. When Coleridge gave the order to return to port, a brief squall overtook them and the boat rocked and tossed like a shuttlecock. By the time the storm subsided, Brian Cummings' skin had turned a greenish white and, with his shock of red hair, he looked like a rare species of tropical bird.

Two hours later, as he staggered down the gangplank, he willed his knees not to buckle, and with obvious reluctance they managed to comply. The stairs to his room in the Grace and Favour were Mount Everest and he finally landed on his bed with a curse on his lips for all patent medicine manufacturers as the phone rang. He just managed to lift the receiver. Into the mouthpiece he gasped, 'Urp', and the sound of Clive Fuller's friendly, fatherly voice almost brought tears to his eyes. The conversation was brief, to the point and one-sided, with Fuller doing all of the talking.

120

In conclusion, Fuller instructed Cummings, 'Get back to me as soon as you can. I'm in for the rest of the evening.'

'Urp,' said Cummings, and hung up. With a herculean effort he rolled over on his stomach, heaved his feet on to the floor, slid off the bed face downward and crawled to the bathroom. He laid his chin on the edge of tub, reached feebly for the red tap and ran the hot water. Where, he wondered unhappily, would he find the strength to make his way to Auriol Kendall's cottage?

Auriol Kendall had sat frowning throughout Owen Farquhar's sermon in church that morning and the sight of her seemingly disapproving face in the front pew had thoroughly unnerved the Vicar. When he noticed her after taking his place in the pulpit, he silently reproached himself for his injudicious choice of theme, Love Thy Neighbour. He delivered it nervously and inarticulately, and at least half his parish were convinced he had breakfasted on sacramental wine.

Auriol heard none of it. She was too deeply absorbed in her own troubled thoughts. The village was buzzing behind her back about Fiona's unusually prolonged absence, and there had been no point in lying about postcards, letters or telegrams. The postmistress had been the first to comment about their strange absence. Although less than twenty-four hours in the future, Monday seemed a century away. She hungered to see Clive Fuller and amend the statement she'd given him. Like the other recipients of Arthur's notes, excepting perhaps the Vicar, she suspected a deeper significance in the incident involving Laura and was thoroughly convinced there was a link with Fiona's disappearance. Wasn't it possible Fiona might be with Laura? *Complete loss of memory*. That could mean Laura forgot Fiona was with her. Absurd. *Absurd*. Fiona stole away on her own with her car and equipment.

The mention of Laura's name brought Auriol out of her deep self-engrossment. The Vicar was announcing Laura's

121

imminent return to the fold and an appreciative murmur echoed through the church. Auriol rummaged in her purse, found a boiled sweet and consigned it to her mouth. From the corner of her eye she saw Emaline Welbeck across the aisle inhaling deeply from a small phial which Auriol assumed contained smelling salts. Her attention reverted to Mr Farquhar as he solemnly told the gathering of Laura's amnesia and said he expected her to be treated with kindness and understanding. The church buzzed like a sawmill at full production. The Vicar raised his hands for silence and when his congregation settled down announced the concluding hymn would be Laura's favourite, 'Abide With Me'. In silent levity Auriol wondered why he lacked the humour to suggest 'Will You Remember?'

At the conclusion, Auriol joined the exciting procession up the centre aisle. She wanted to be out of the door before the Vicar took his usual Sunday position there. She felt a tug at her sleeve and glanced over her shoulder.

'Any word from Fiona?' Emaline Welbeck inquired in a faint voice.

Auriol squared her shoulders. 'None whatsoever.'

'How unkind of her,' sympathised Emaline. 'If it will be of any comfort, you're welcome to come look at her statue any time you like.'

'Thank you,' said Auriol through clenched teeth, grimly bringing to mind a similar offer made by Emaline to Dr Kettering after Viola's death. 'I suppose Frank's eagerly looking forward to resuming work on Charlotte Corday with Laura.'

'You'll have to ask him,' said Emaline stonily, 'we haven't been speaking.' It came as no surprise to Auriol. Prolonged silences between the battling Welbecks were as regular as the seasons.

'Why don't you go off on a little holiday?' suggested Auriol. 'Absence makes the heart grow fonder.' Even as she spoke, she felt a little stab under her left breast which she attributed to Fiona.

'I can't leave Frank,' said Emaline like the commander of a fort under siege.

'I'm sure Laura will change everything,' said Auriol with a false cheerfulness that emerged flatter than her most recent souffle. 'I know *I* can't wait to see her.'

'Don't you think she'll be staying in seclusion for a while? After all there'll be Arthur for heaven's sake, and the private nurse and . . . and that detective person.' They had reached the end of the aisle and Emaline drew Auriol to one side. 'Auriol, have you any idea what *really* went on at Laura's *that* night?'

'None whatsoever.'

'There must be more to it than we've been told. I saw the constables poking around there again yesterday afternoon.'

'Where?'

'Laura's cottage.'

'What were *you* doing there?'

'I check it every so often to see no one's broken in. It's the neighbourly thing to do.'

'Very neighbourly.'

'What do you suppose they're looking for?'

'Who?'

'The constables!'

Auriol gave it some thought. 'Perhaps Laura's lost an earring.'

Emaline stared at the floor. 'I wish Laura wasn't coming back.'

'That's not very neighbourly.'

'I mean with the others,' Emaline amended hastily. 'It's all so mysterious. I think that's what's unnerving Frank. He's even taken to sleeping in the studio since Arthur's note came.'

'Oh, Emaline,' said Auriol impatiently, while wondering how to avoid a confrontation with the Vicar 'he always does that when you two fall out. It's never bothered you before. Come, come, Emaline, I've always admired your

123

strength. How anyone could put up with Frank's tempera-
ment . . .'

'Don't you dare say a word against him!'

'I have never said a word against your brother,' said
Auriol, pointedly thrusting her head forward until their
noses almost met, 'even when I have had cause to.'

Emaline reared back and folded her arms with a stern
expression. 'What do you mean by *that*?'

'I don't chew my fat twice,' said Auriol and moved past
Emaline towards the door.

What did she mean by *that*, Emaline repeated to herself.
Does she suspect what I suspect? I wonder. She's unnatur-
ally calm about Fiona. She seems to find nothing unusual in
this detective person returning with Laura. Why, I have a
feeling she's looking forward to it. Emaline's eyes narrowed. I think she knows something she's not telling, the
way I'm *positive* Ed Kettering knows. He was called to the
cottage. But he won't discuss it. No matter how much I pry
and prod, he won't discuss it. Oh, dear God. She looked at
the ceiling in supplication and gave silent thanks that over
her head was no sign of a Damoclean sword. She moved her
head towards the door and saw Auriol Kendall rudely
ignore the Vicar's somewhat weak greeting. What was *that*
all about, she wondered.


Laura didn't sleep after Nurse Murdock departed with
the tray of uneaten food. She couldn't have been more wide
awake. She propped herself up on the bed, drew up her
knees and reached for the notebook and pencil. For ten
minutes she appended to her copious notes the fruit of her
cross-examination of Nurse Murdock. Telephone torn from
wall. Alone on couch at least half an hour. Isn't it possible
someone else might have entered the cottage in Arthur's
absence? Surely from time to time people drop in on me
unannounced. Was I really holding the knife when Arthur
found me in the kitchen, and if not, why is he lying? If
Arthur does hate me as I so strongly suspect, is our estrange-

ment sufficient reason?

She looked up at the blank wall opposite which reflected a mental image of Arthur leering at her with fervent distaste. She found it extremely unattractive and resumed writing.

If Fiona was a witness to the murder, why did she run away? Why didn't she report it? Why didn't she go for help? Why didn't she tell Auriol? Or is she shielding someone? *Good heavens,* underlining both words heavily, perhaps it's Fiona who *hates me,* even more heavily underlined. If so, why did she spend the night. Even more so, why did I *let her* spend the night? Would I know or suspect her loathing?

She looked up at the wall again. She saw Fiona ringed by a halo of fluttering butterflies looking extremely bland. If it was telling her Fiona didn't hate her, she was delighted to agree. She returned to the notebook.

Very carefully she printed, 'Leave Harborford Or I'll Kill You.' Since the note was found in my dress pocket, had I shown it to Fiona? Had it come through the mail? Was it slipped under my door? Or was the note . . .

Her hand froze. *Of course!*

'Oh, damn you, Clive Fuller!' she shouted at the wall. 'You've probably been thinking this all along *too*!' Damn you, Clive Fuller, she repeated to herself as she dialled his home number. She let the phone ring twenty times and then slammed it back on the receiver in anger and frustration.

*Damn you, Clive Fuller!*

At twilight, Auriol Kendall sat in a wicker chair on her front lawn sipping her fourth double dry martini. The wicker table on her right held vodka, vermouth, a pitcher and stirrer, and a small red bucket of ice. Behind the bucket was a jar of boiled sweets. She wore a pale yellow Japanese kimono loosely tied with a purple obi, suitable attire to match the suicidal feeling which had come over her after returning from church. She felt abandoned, unwanted, unnecessary, unloved and unkempt. After her brief conversation with Emaline, she had a chilling feeling she might never see Fiona again, and without Fiona she felt life was purposeless.

She had wept into her lonely bowl of scotch broth at lunch, and now for the third time that day tried to recall the last drunken argument with Fiona.

She knows. She *must* know. But how? How?

She banged the arm of the wicker chair with a strong fist, drained the glass and then hazily leaned over to bring number five into the world.

If she knows, even if she suspects, is that enough to drive her away from me *forever*? Couldn't she have spared me some *compassion*? After all, I'm her ... she sloshed vodka on to the table and with an effort leaned over and sponged it with her tongue. Settled again with the fifth martini, she rubbed the inside of a thigh.

I have failings too, Fiona. I have had my lapses. Do not condemn me for them. I only tried to spare you a shocking tragedy. Oh, God ... *God* ... if only I had someone to talk to!

And like a sign from heaven she saw in the distance, on the road that went past the cottage, a beautiful flash of red bobbing along just barely visible over the tall hedges. She leaned forward and squinted. The flash of red was beautiful, beautiful enough for her to have mixed on the palette. Then the flash of red passed the hedges, and she saw it was a flaming shock of hair capping a tall young man with dead white skin. He was clutching the fence that circled her property and stopped to take a deep breath. He seemed unsteady on his feet. Auriol struggled forward in the chair and called out, 'Are you ill, young man?'

Brian Cummings turned in the direction of the voice and prayed what he saw was Auriol Kendall.

'Been out fishing!' he called back shakily. 'I guess I'm still a little seasick! Thought I could walk it off!'

'Oh, you poor dear thing! I have just the remedy! A nice ice cold double dry vodka martini!'

It was twilight when an anxious Laura finally connected with Fuller. After three hours of no reply during which Nurse Murdock had brought her a snack of tea and cucumber sandwiches, now cold, dry, unsipped and uneaten, she had the added frustration of an interminable engaged signal. When the connection was finally made and she heard Fuller's 'Hello?', she said with undisguised irritation, 'It's Laura here and don't say anything, just listen. It's that damn note you found in my dress pocket! Now see here, Clive, it certainly must have dawned on you. Just because it was found in my pocket doesn't necessarily mean it was meant for *me*!'

Fuller was smiling into his brandy and soda.

'Clive, are you listening?'

'I am.'

'Well then, if Fiona Cooper was at the house with me, couldn't the bloody note have been sent to *Fiona*?'

'What took you so long?' he inquired matter-of-factly.

## Chapter Eleven

Fuller almost dropped the phone as Laura's shriek of anger pierced his eardrum. When it was back at his ear, he could hear her furiously cataloguing the information she had had to ferret out for herself, and was this his idea of sportsmanship? If Laura Denning is supposed to be endowed with unique deductive powers and they were supposed to be co-operating then what the hell was the big idea? Oh, certainly she understands that in the eyes of the law she's undoubtedly guilty of this anonymous crime until proven innocent, or is it supposed to be the other way around, and

127

she doesn't give two figs if it is, but just *think* of how many innocent people have suffered execution in the past and here she sits (she was actually reclining with a half-eaten apple) with a splitting headache due to anxiety and mental strain and was undoubtedly on the verge of a relapse and, oh yes, had he checked if Fiona Cooper was back in Harborford?

She had apparently paused for breath so Fuller said swiftly into the mouthpiece, 'I'm glad to see my therapy is working.'

'What therapy?' she barked back.

'I'm hoping the more you're forced to think for yourself the sooner the veil will lift.'

'Oh.'

'As to Fiona Cooper, I'm waiting to hear from Brian Cummings. I was speaking to Brian if you were wondering why my line was engaged earlier.'

'Oh.'

'As to your other clever conjectures, being alone in the cottage and the possibility of the knife having been placed in your hand then which means your husband could be lying, that is all under consideration.'

She felt like an applicant for a secretarial position. 'I think I'll call Arthur on that right *now*!'

'I'd prefer you didn't,' he cautioned her anxiously. 'The question will be put to him in Harborford, and in my own good time. Now why don't you ring Nurse Murdock?'

'What for?'

'Aspirin for your headache.'

'What headache? Oh! Yes . . . thank you, I will. Well . . . I suppose that's all.'

'Until tomorrow morning.'

'Yes.'

'Oh . . . and Laura . . . !'

Her heart quickened. 'Yes?'

'Pleasant dreams.'

He gently lowered the phone on to the receiver. He wondered in what octave she would respond when he eventually told Laura of having her nightmare analysed.

Laura studied the half-eaten apple. She imagined it had the size and contour of Clive Fuller's head. She bit into it ferociously.


'There's nothing like a double dry vodka martini to bring the colour back to one's cheeks!' Auriol piped. Brian was about to suggest a blood transfusion could have the same effect, but thought better of it. They had moved inside to the sitting room after Auriol complained of a chill, Brian carrying the cocktail ingredients and Auriol tripping lightly ahead of him.

Brian's cheeks were flushed but not because of vodka. Auriol was darting about the room switching on lamps, the kimono flapping loosely and revealing more of Auriol than anyone had seen since her gall stone operation. 'Aren't they beautiful!' exclaimed Brian and Auriol hastily drew the kimono tighter around her breasts until she realised he was examining Fiona's cases of butterflies which covered two walls.

'They're Fiona's,' said Auriol a bit coldly, 'she's a lepi-dopterist.'

'Fiona?' The innocence in Brian's voice might have won an acquittal for Bluebeard.

'My niece. She lives here.'

'Oh, she does?' said Brian brightly. 'I'd like to meet her.'

'She's away.' This was information Brian might just have easily unearthed over a beer at the inn, but there was more to his assignment from Clive Fuller. Brian's group had been cautioned not to arouse suspicion in the village. They were to behave as any ordinary fishing party would until Fuller's arrival. And Fuller wanted as much fresh in-formation as possible about Fiona's relationships with Laura Denning's circle of friends before the helicopter arrived the next morning. Having met Auriol Kendall,

129

Brian was not relishing the assignment.

Auriol was stirring her sixth. 'I was thinking about her just as you appeared on the road. Young man, I must say you are heaven sent.' Brian was flattened against a wall, and except for the absence of a pin through his midriff, resembled a new species of butterfly. 'I was just praying for somebody to talk to.' He moved away from the wall and edged towards a sideboard which he leaned against, he hoped, nonchalantly. From the opposite side of the room, Auriol's thickening tongue struggled to enunciate. 'She's been gone over a month now, and not a word! Not a word!'

Brian suggested with feigned concern, 'Does she do this often?'

'Never!' Brian felt the floor shaking.

'You should report her to missing persons.'

'Tomorrow,' said Auriol, weaving towards the couch, carefully holding the martini in front of her like a sacred icon. 'There's a very famous detective coming to stay with a friend tomorrow. I read a book he wrote.' She had lowered herself on to the couch. 'I'm sure you've heard of my friend. Laura Denning?'

'Oh yes!' said Cummings with the eagerness of an autograph hunter cornering the elusive Garbo. 'Is *she* your friend?' He struck oil. Auriol launched into a recital of the Laura incident, from the night of Fiona's disappearance through Arthur's note to the next day's expected return during which she invitingly patted the seat next to her and after a moment's hesitation during which he reminded himself this was the line of duty, he crossed the room and sat down stiffly.

'Oh, Fiona, Fiona,' she suddenly wailed, 'my child of love!' Her right palm landed on his left knee and he fought to keep a muscle from twitching.

'Child of love,' he managed to say, 'that's very touching.'

Auriol's head swivelled to him and he could tell she was having trouble focusing. 'Did *I* say child of love?' Brian

130

nodded and Auriol found a smile. 'I love her very much, the wicked thing. Uh ... she's my brother's child. My brother Rodney.'

'Oh well then, perhaps she's gone to stay with her parents. Have you thought of contacting them?'

'I'd need a seance for that. They've been dead thirty years!' She took a gulp of martini and then continued. 'Rodney and Cynthia were missionaries. They were killed in the Amazon.' Brian was fascinated. 'Headhunters, I was told. Can't imagine *anyone* wanting to collect their heads, they were so unattractive.' She stared into the martini. 'I brought up Fiona. I worked all my adult life to support her and educate her at the convent.' She looked up and announced her artistic profession like the second coming. Brian acted duly impressed. 'I'm in my gladiola period now.'

'How long have you lived here?' inquired Brian, while wondering if he dared tempt the fates with a second cocktail.

'Years,' said Auriol in a ghostly whisper, 'years and years and years. Twenty-eight of them to be precise.' She pronounced precise *prethithe* but was totally unaware of it. 'There was a war then, and this once was a sort of artist's colony. I knew Frank Welbeck. Did you realise we'd been at art school together?' Brian said he didn't. 'Well, that's where we met. I was a young widow then. Married less than a year and a widow.' She clucked her tongue. 'God was I lucky. Frank's estate is next to mine.' She jerked her head in what Cummings assumed was the direction of the Welbeck estate, and he felt her hair brush against his ear. His knee was burning where her palm still rested and he wondered if the palm would move with his leg if he attempted to cross it. 'So you're here fishing!'

'What?'

'Fishing! Fishing!'

'Oh yes! Fishing! That's right, with four chums. Is that Frank Welbeck the *sculptor*?'

'Yeth.' She made strange noises as she tasted her tongue with displeasure and then her face relaxed. 'He was going to be a painter when I met him. But Emaline had other ideas.' She explained Emaline while Brian stifled a yawn. He was hearing as yet nothing new about Emaline. 'I suppose Frank has her to thank for guiding him to sculpture,' she said ruefully, 'but it's cost him his freedom. *She's* the one with the money, you know. Got it all. The father never liked Frank. Would you mix me another, dear? I feel glued here.' Brian was grateful for the reprieve, took her glass and moved to the bar with alacrity.

'It's unnatural,' he heard her say over the decanting vodka.

'What is?' he asked.

'Emaline and Frank. Very unhealthy. I'm well out of it.'

His ears perked. 'Well out of what?'

'What do you mean by that?' she asked suspiciously.

'You said you were well out of it and I asked well out of what.'

'I haven't the vaguest idea what you're talking about.' She fell back against the sofa. 'Oh, Fiona, Fiona! We had such a terrible argument that Thunday.' Brian wanted to keep her talking. He was afraid he might lose her any moment to an alcoholic stupor.

'How much vermouth?'

'Just glare at the bottle and bring me the drink. And you have another too. I can't *stand* drinking alone when I have company.' He mixed himself a light one.

'I'm sure you've argued before,' he said as he returned with the drinks.

'Sure we have. But *that* one ... it was *awful*!' She buried her face in her hands and rocked. Brian took the opportunity to pull up a chair and sit across from her. Auriol lifted her head and addressed the empty space on her right. 'We said terrible things to each other ... where *are* you?'

'Just over here.' He held her drink out. She took it with both hands.

'There's a man,' said Auriol darkly as she guided the glass to her mouth. 'I'm positive there's a man. Oh, God, if it's Frank . . . oh, God . . .' God dissolved into a gargle as she drank. Brian's eye caught the photo of Auriol and Fiona.

'Is that Fiona with you in the picture?'

'Yeth.'

'She's very attractive.'

'Yeth.'

'Why, Welbeck must be old enough to be her father.'

'Yeth.'

'She wouldn't be involved with a man that old.'

'Howda *you* know?' she asked belligerently.

'I don't know. I just don't think she would, that's all.'

'Well, Emaline thinkth otherwithe! But Emaline thinkth that about every woman Frank meeth. Am I lithping?'

'I'm afraid you are, yes.'

She chuckled. 'Vodka thickens my tongue.'

And loosens it, Brian thought gratefully. 'Aren't Fiona and Emaline friends?'

'I suppose so. They play cards, that's friendly. But you never know with Emaline. Emaline loves Laura. That's who Emaline loves. And that's funny, because I'm *positive* it's been Frank and Laura . . . *positive*!' Clive Fuller might not know the more private contents of Laura's notebook, but Brian did. Elaine Murdock shared everything with this husband she passionately adored, and the thought of an affair between Laura and the elderly Welbeck made Brian uncomfortable. 'You're wiggling!' announced Auriol, 'Come back here!' She slammed a hand down on the couch. Brian obeyed. 'You know what?'

'What?'

'I'm going to paint your portrait!'

'Oh, how very kind of you.'

'You look like a chrysanthemum, so it should be easy.

133

You'll find my palette and paints in the kitchen.'

'You mean now?'

'Of course now!'

'But in this light?'

'Love,' she leaned forward seductively, 'you'd look good in any light.'

'Oh . . . now . . . well . . . er . . . Mrs *Kendall* . . . the drink . . . it's spilling all over me. . . . *Mrs Kendall* . . . please . . . your nails . . . they're so *sharp*. . . . Mrs *Kendall*!'


'Frank?' Emaline scratched gently at the studio door. 'Please answer me, Frank!'

He sat on the crate leaning forward with his hands pressed together at the palms, staring at a trough of freshly mixed plaster of paris.

'Frank! Are you in there?'

He heard the door rattle and put his hands over his ears.

'*Frank!* Your dinner's getting cold! You haven't eaten all day! Frank! You'll be *sick*!'

He folded his arms and stared at the incompleted statue of Charlotte Corday, blinking his eyes as though fighting back tears.

'This can't go on, Frank! They'll be here tomorrow! How will it look to *them* if we continue acting like this towards each other? Damn you, you stubborn idiot! Come out of there!'

He got to his feet, thrust his hands into his trouser pockets, and slowly began circling Charlotte Corday.

'Fra-a-a-ank-ieeee! I've got ham hocks and beans and water cress salad with your fayyyyyy . . . vourite dressing . . .' Her voice rose and fell like a school mistress reading a fairy tale to a kindergarden class. '. . . and trifle with cherries and . . .'

He picked up a chisel and hurled it at the door.

Her voice hardened. 'You're a damned fool. You're a damned *fool*, Frank. Who were you talking to on the phone when I got back from church?' She pounded on the door.

'Who was it?' There was no response. 'Well I *know* who it was, see?' She stood with her fists on her hips, her face contorted venomously. 'I called Enid at the switchboard and she told me it was London! *London!*'

'Get away, Medusa.' His voice slid under the door, encircled her body and scratched at her ears like a rasp.

'Come out of there!'

'Away with you!' he shouted, 'or I smash this one to smithereens!'

'Noooooo!' she screeched frantically, 'Noooooo! Oh, Frankie ... Frankie ... I prayed for us in church ... I prayed for *us*! Oh, God,' she implored the darkening sky, 'Oh, God, where are you? Emaline's a good girl! Emaline loves her brother! Why won't you make him speak to Emaline? Do you still blame Emaline for one *naughty* mistake?'

Frank rushed to the door and kicked it.

'God, where are you?' demanded Emaline. 'I have suffered *enough*!'

'Hypocrite!' thundered Frank Welbeck from behind the door, 'bloody hypocrite! I'll eat when I'm hungry and I'm not hungry so get away from here! I'm trying to finish this stinking statue!'

Her face brightened. 'You *are* darling? Oh, that's my good brother. That's my darling brother. All right. Frank? I'm going away, Frank.' She hugged herself with joy as she retraced her steps to the kitchen door. He's finishing Charlotte Corday! At last! He's back at work again after all these terrible weeks. Good old Frank. Good old brother.

Frank would have to mix a fresh batch of plaster of paris. He was vomiting into the trough.

The fireplace was blazing in the saloon of the Grace and Favour though it was a balmy night. The blazing fireplace was a tradition and some joked the staff was kept busy overnight keeping the blaze alive. Brian's four companions were scattered through the room, two playing darts, one

135

engaging the bartender in conversation and the fourth seated near Edmund Kettering and Sean Coleridge, straining to overhear their conversation. What snatches he caught told him Coleridge was again attempting to draw the Doctor out about what he really knew of the incident at the cottage. He knew as much as the Doctor did which was more than Coleridge knew, and hoped the conversation would steer towards more intimate details about Laura Denning's friends.

After an hour and three rounds of whiskies for them, two bitters for him, he learned little more than the fact that both men were rivals for Mrs Denning's attentions and didn't much relish Arthur Denning's impending presence. After a while he could sense Coleridge was growing bored with the Doctor, which he fully appreciated, as the Doctor was growing mawkish over Laura Denning and her friendship with the Doctor's late wife. He overheard the Doctor mention Frank Welbeck in connection with Viola Kettering's posing for the statue of Catherine de Medici and out of the corner of his eye thought he detected a significant change of expression in Coleridge's face which the doctor apparently didn't notice.

The young man, whose name was Aubrey Lewis, found himself wondering if Coleridge suspected or perhaps positively knew of a possible liaison between the sculptor and the dead woman. At least that was *something* for Clive Fuller, slim though it be. He hoped Brian Cummings was faring better with Auriol Kendall. Then he saw Brian in the hallway quickly walking past the entrance to the saloon, for some strange reason shielding his face with a handkerchief, apparently heading for his room. He thought of following Brian to ask him if he'd got any results, when he heard Edmund Kettering speak Fiona's name and signalled for his third bitter.

Clive Fuller, in dressing-gown and slippers, sat in an easy chair next to the phone, puffing the pipe and con-

136

tentedly listening to a Haydn Symphony on the Hi-Fi. The music was helping to calm his impatience to hear from Brian Cummings. When the second movement began, the phone rang. He told Brian to hold on while he turned off the music, and then returned to his seat and listened to Brian, whose voice sounded uncomfortably strained, repeat the information he had gleaned from Auriol Kendall about herself and Fiona. Fuller had a pad on his knee and made notes. Finally, an amused expression crossed his face as Brian told him of Auriol's intention to paint his portrait. The expression froze as Brian told him what followed.

'You're joking!'

'I am *not*,' came Brian's indignant and pained reply, 'she tried to *rape* me!' Fuller could hear the phone rattling in Cummings' hand.

'Get on with it, Brian,' said Fuller impatiently, 'what did you do?'

Brian dabbed at the scratches on his face and felt perspiration beading on his forehead. 'I tried to reason with her, but it was impossible. She was like a lioness! I struggled out of her grip . . .' he paused to lick his lips, 'she had me on the couch then . . .' Fuller exhaled, '. . . I raced for the door. But so help me, Clive, she may be over fifty but she let go with a flying tackle and we tumbled to the floor of the hall. It was awful!'

Fuller's legs were sprawled out in front of him and the pipe hung limply from his left hand.

'I don't know how long we rolled around there. But her kimono came undone and she kept yelling, "Kiss me you fool!" and I told her I was a married man and she said so what, every man cheats the beasts or something like that, and I finally got a grip on her waist and scrambled to my feet and got the door open, but she had a hammerlock on my ankle, all the time struggling up, and I bent over to try and loosen her fingers. My God they were like a vice and she reached up and scratched my face. How do I explain this to Elaine?'

137

'Calm down, calm down,' said Fuller, 'she's probably embarrassed about the whole thing by now or will be when she sobers up if she remembers.'

'But you don't understand,' sobbed Cummings, 'when she started tearing at my face I just lost all control of myself. Oh my God, Clive . . . *I hit her*!'

Fuller groaned and rubbed his forehead.

'Wouldn't this be considered the line of duty?' Brian pleaded into the phone.

Fuller drew his legs up and crossed them. Would Auriol Kendall dare bring a charge of assault against the redheaded detective and risk becoming a laughing stock in the village once the facts of the incident were revealed in court. He doubted it. Feeling reassured, he began to enjoy himself immensely. 'Was she unconscious when you left her?'

'I don't think so,' Cummings told him, dabbing at the perspiration with the blood-stained handkerchief, unaware his forehead was now streaked like an Indian brave's. 'She was lying there in the hall, flat on her back, eyes open and breathing heavily.'

'Probably still in the throes of passion,' commented Fuller drily. 'Tell you what, clean yourself up, contact the local constables, explain the situation and I'm sure they'll know how to handle it.'

'Clive?'

'Yes?'

'Will you explain it to Elaine please? I mean sort of prepare her?'

'I think Elaine is prepared for anything. Good night Brian.'

'Good night. Thank you.'

Fuller checked and rechecked the information gleaned from Auriol Kendall. He felt there was at least one answer staring him in the face, but he couldn't find it. He knew something pertinent to Fiona Cooper was there, something the young woman might have shared that night with Laura Denning, but his deductive dowsing rod wasn't responding.

He started again at the beginning, puffing heavily on the pipe. *Auriol Kendall and Frank Welbeck were art students together.* He thought of the Bible. 'In the beginning . . .'

## Chapter Twelve

Brian Cummings washed his face, applied a styptic pencil to the scratches on his face and was changing into slacks and turtle-neck sweater when the phone rang. The voice at the other end was coyly girlish and slightly slurred.

'Naughty boy, plying me with so many martinis.' He caught his breath. 'That is *you*, isn't it Mr Cummings?'

'Yes, ma'am,' he squeaked.

He heard a sigh of relief. 'Forgive me for falling asleep the way I did, but it's been an exhausting day. Now how's your tummy.'

It was turning somersaults but he wasn't about to tell her. 'Much better, thank you.'

'Oh, I'm *so* glad. I just wanted to make sure you're home safely. It's such a long walk to the village.'

'I enjoy walking.'

'Oh, *so* do I! Well thank you again for such a pleasant evening. And now that you know the way, don't be a stranger.'

'No, ma'am.'

'*Ma'am.* How quaint. Good night.'

Brian fell back across the bed and murmured over and over to himself, 'There is a God Thank you God There is a God Thank you God. . . .'

It was after midnight when Emaline Welbeck, sitting in a rocker in the library, staring at the ashes in the fireplace, heard her brother enter the house and go upstairs to his room. A sly smile played on her lips as she left the chair, picked up a poker, and began stirring the ashes.

*I know who it was, see! It was London! London!*

She revived an ember into a tiny flame and it seemed to hold her hypnotised. The reflection of the flame danced in her eyes and Emaline began to hum. In the flame she was seeing a vision. Frank and Emaline entering Buckingham Palace. Frank and Emaline presented to the Queen. And then the investiture. The dream of three decades come true.

*Sir* Frank Welbeck.

Emaline smiled her crooked smile at the flame. It will happen. Nothing, no one, will stand in the way of that. It is my only dream, my one precious dream. It will come true.

Unlike Emaline's dream, the flame died.

It was after midnight and Arthur Denning sat at the desk in the library of the flat which he and Laura had taken such pride in furnishing. He wrote, scratched out, rewrote and sipped brandy. He stared at the bottle and remembered in the past three hours he'd consumed more than half. Have I had dinner? He couldn't recall, yet he felt sober. His handwriting seemed clear. His mind was alert. It must be. His grammar was impeccable. His syntax was admirable. If he were double-jointed, he'd pat himself on the back, but then there was the danger of stabbing himself with the pen. Why not, he thought. In one area and one area alone was he a member of a majority. He didn't like himself.

He re-read carefully the three pages he had filled and was satisfied. He opened the centre drawer of the desk for a fresh piece of paper and saw the gun. For the fourth time that night he checked the magazine and satisfied himself it was loaded. He placed the gun on the desk at the base of a framed photograph of Laura. Laura was smiling. Laura looked pleased. He had done nothing to please Laura in years. He wanted one last opportunity to please her again.

He resumed writing.

It was after midnight and archaic licensing laws be damned, drinks were still being served in the saloon of the Grace and Favour. Mr Rigby, the innkeeper, wasn't worried about the possibility of a fine being imposed. His son was one of the village constables. He was behind the bar helping his father. There were a dozen men present including Sean Coleridge, Edmund Kettering, Brian Cummings and his four companions. Brian had explained away the scratches on his face with a lavish fabrication of a walk along the cliff and a near-perilous fall. The group was boisterous and dirty jokes spun and lit up the room like a catherine wheel.

'My round!' shouted Brian and bowed from the waist to the cheers. Aubrey Lewis clutched the bar to keep from falling and Brian cautioned him, 'Steady, mate.' Lewis's mouth twisted into a Stan Laurel grin as he raised his glass.

'Laura Denning!'

Dr Kettering's eyes darted to the left and found Sean Coleridge. Both had seen Brian's elbow connect with Lewis's lower rib. Neither spoke. There was nothing to say. There was no need to. Unseen by them, Brian winked at Lewis and Lewis shouted, 'My round!'

It was after midnight and Elaine Murdock was neatly packing her suitcase between sips of milk and nibbles of chocolate biscuits. She packed freshly starched uniforms, underclothes and stockings, three dresses, several pairs of trousers, blouses and sweaters, a first aid kit and a service revolver.

It was after midnight and Laura Denning lay in bed wide awake and staring at the ceiling. The night lamp glowed and pencil and notebook rested on her chest. There had been another phone conversation with Clive Fuller, though he had done most of the talking while she busily took notes. They shared a laugh at Brian and Auriol Kendall's expense, briefly discussed the information imparted by Fuller, said their good nights, and now Laura couldn't sleep.

*Maybe it's the moon over Cornwall....*

Laura groped for the notebook, lifted it and blocked the ceiling. Auriol Frank Emaline Fiona headhunters art school argument Laura and how, she wondered, do these names and words tie together? Man. Fiona and Man? Fiona and Which Man? Frank and Emaline. Unnatural. Laura exhaled and rolled over on her stomach, felt the pencil and raised herself to extract it.

Suddenly she was thinking of Dame Marjorie and the overheard argument. Fiona and Welbeck. Fiona and Welbeck? What the hell, it's a start. Her mind clicked like a camera shutter and there was Arthur. What do *you* want, Arthur? Arthur refused to budge. She shrugged and wrote his name.

Fiona and Welbeck and Arthur.

She studied the sentence and felt something was wrong with it. She studied harder, thought, and then pencilled out a word and a name.

Fiona and Arthur.

*Fiona and Arthur?*

She propped herself up on an elbow, tapped the pad furiously with the pencil and stared at the phone.

*Fiona and Arthur?*

It was after midnight and Clive Fuller was listening to Beethoven on the Hi-Fi. His notes were voluminous and his eyes ached with the strain. The phone rang and he glared at the instrument. On the third ring he lifted it and heard Laura breathlessly inquire 'I haven't awakened you, have I?' He assured her she hadn't and she spoke rapidly and he listened patiently. Towards the finish she inquired anxiously, 'Well, what do you think? Do you suppose for some of those field trips we can read *London*?'

'Anything's possible.'

'I had to tell you now. I was afraid there'd be no chance

142

tomorrow morning what with Arthur there. Shall we spring it on him?' she asked with an almost perverse-sounding delight.

'We don't spring anything on anyone yet,' he said somewhat sharply, which made her instantly regret the underlying frivolity in her suggestion.

'I didn't mean that the way it sounded, Clive,' she said.

'I hope you didn't.' It must be the hour, Laura hoped, he's never spoken to me with such severity before. The same thought might have occurred to him and his voice softened. 'We're dealing with human beings, not chess pieces. They have to be studied and understood and sympathised with. Murder doesn't evolve from a diagram. The root of murder is emotion, an emotion stronger than love. You can treat Arthur and the others like ciphers, but ciphers don't always add up. Tomorrow begins the most delicate and dangerous part of this operation. Is this sinking in or are you doing your nails?'

'Now who's being frivolous? My case of opening night nerves is as bad as yours. I know Arthur's human, that's why I find it conceivable he may be or has been involved with Fiona. I'm trying to lay out as much as possible before we board that helicopter tomorrow morning. I'm trying to pinpoint a logical reason for Fiona's spending that night with me and if it has any connection with my phoning Arthur. Maybe Arthur is why she and Auriol argued.'

'Maybe isn't good enough,' he replied while struggling to prop the phone between his shoulder and ear and light the pipe.

'What about that photo I took of Auriol and Fiona?' she said hotly.

'What about it?'

'At first glance you thought Fiona was me! Isn't that what you told me?'

'I did.'

'Didn't you make some comment on that to Auriol?'

'Of course not. It wasn't important then. You'd be surprised what one misses in the first stages of an investigation.' He added with a twinkle in his voice. 'Even Hercule Poirot isn't infallible.'

'Oh, I give up!' She flung her notebook aside and ran her hand through her hair.

'You're forgetting the information Brian Cummings got from Auriol. She didn't harp on Arthur, she harped on Frank Welbeck.'

'Oh,' said Laura with renewed interest as she struggled to an upright position. 'Auriol might think it's Frank and Fiona. And Auriol might have a case on Welbeck herself.'

'Try that in the past tense.'

'Try what?'

'Auriol might have *had* a case on Welbeck, years back when they first met as art students. Auriol says they met after she was widowed. But that's what Auriol says. I think it might have happened before that. She could have married on the rebound.'

Laura brightened considerably. 'Of course! If Auriol thought Fiona was having an affair she'd naturally assume it was with someone in the neighbourhood. She'd never consider Arthur because he hasn't been around for quite a while. It probably hasn't occured to her Fiona could be sneaking off to London to see him!'

'Congratulations!'

'Great! So why don't we spring it on Arthur tomorrow?'

Fuller groaned, 'Go right *ahead*. *Spring* it on Arthur! Then what? Arthur easily denies it because unless he admits it freely you have no proof, he thickens his guard and then we might *never* reach him. We *need* Arthur. He's our most important link in this chain. You treat him with indifference when you should be breaking your back winning his confidence!'

'Go ahead,' she interjected venomously.

'I have every intention. We suspect Arthur knows more than he's told, right?'

'*Right.*'

The word stung and he shuddered, then shook his head to clear it and continued. 'I think Arthur plays mute because he's in a bind. He's torn between loyalties, you and probably Fiona. There's certainly more to it than that but I don't see it. It's inside Arthur. It's a part of his make-up. He's confused and frightened. Why do you suppose he visited Mater this morning? It's quite obvious they don't like each other, but she's a powerful woman. He goes to her presumably to warn her against a possible scandal. We mustn't be as naive about Dame Marjorie as Arthur is. She's bloody smart. She knows what he's really hoping is that with her influence she'll do something about quashing the entire affair. The easy way out. But not our Dame Marjorie. She's been around too long. This incident took place in a small village, and small villages whisper and whispers grow loud and spread. Whispers never die down. Dame Marjorie is smart enough to realise that, so she wants the matter settled fast and then sit back and wait for it to become yesterday's news. Thank goodness she's also terribly fond of *you*. Are you *there*?'

'Where's to go?' she inquired sweetly.

'You've been so quiet,' he grumbled.

'I'm all ears. Do go on.' The notebook was back on her lap and she was doodling.

'Tomorrow morning Arthur's the reluctant passenger. He can't face that cottage again. He doesn't want to go back to Harborford because he's afraid when you and he appear in the flesh, something will come to a boil and erupt.'

The doodling had stopped. The hand that held the pencil was now shielding her eyes as she felt faint. He had paused to let his words sink in, but now the extended silence gave him concern.

'Laura? Laura are you all right?'

She summoned her voice with an effort. 'You've made me realise something that's left me a bit drained. Clive . . . you think Arthur might know the assailant's identity.'

'Yes.'

'Yes,' she repeated with loathing. 'And he's let me suffer this hell.'

'I don't think intentionally.'

'Then *why*?' She held the phone so tightly she thought it might crack.

'Why were you so anxious to establish the fact you were alone in the cottage for half an hour while Arthur rushed to summon Dr Kettering?'

'Because I think *that's* when the knife was placed in my hand.'

'Full marks for you. Now here's what I think is Arthur's involvement. Listen carefully.'

'You know I am!' she snapped.

'I think when Arthur arrived at the cottage, the murder had already been committed and the body removed . . . *but someone was in the kitchen with you.*'

'Removing the fingerprints?'

'Probably. Whoever that person was, they said something to the effect they happened to drop in and just *look* at this carnage, hurry for a doctor, Arthur, look at poor Laura and the state she's in, you can't phone because it's torn from the wall. Remember now, Arthur is in a complete panic. You might have mentioned Fiona when you phoned, and there is no sign of Fiona. He carries you into the sitting room, places you on the couch all the time wondering what's become of Fiona. Perhaps he wonders aloud and the other person goes tearing off presumably to alert Fiona. Arthur doesn't know what to think or do because he doesn't do either easily in a crisis, so the most obvious act is to get Kettering.

'He goes tearing off. You're alone. I think that other person slipped back into the house, placed the knife in your hand, and when Arthur returned with Kettering he stupidly thought he was in an inextricable trap. There you were now holding the knife. Can he be sure who put it there? The person he encountered earlier or someone else? Perhaps *Fiona*! He undoubtedly felt he couldn't say anything to

Kettering. Anything he does or says could be a dangerous blunder. There's you, there's Fiona, there's his mother, there's himself. He sees four worlds exploding. He could have a suspicion but certainly no proof as to how the knife got there.

'According to Kettering he returned to the village to summon the constable and phone Dr Flint and myself at Arthur's request. What Arthur's doing in the interim is complete conjecture. But I think he may have sought out the person he found in the kitchen earlier, and somehow that confrontation led to his subsequent silence, with the hope that somehow, by some miracle, it will all blow over. When you awaken with amnesia, he feels even more secure. But in the meantime he's apparently had no word from Fiona. His confusion worsens. Who is a murderer? You? Fiona? The person he encountered in the kitchen? Or even worse . . . *was Fiona murdered*?'

He sucked on the pipe, but it was dead.

Laura cleared her throat. 'Well, that's a fascinating theory.'

'Thank you. But let me repeat, I have been wrong before. Have I impressed on you how much we need Arthur?'

Laura's eyes narrowed and she spoke with suspicion. 'Have you just made all this up?'

'I'm good, but not all that good. I've been playing with this for days and I feel I'm close. Given time and kindness, I think Arthur will break. That's your job.'

'I'm not a very good actress, but I'll do my best. I'd better prepare you for something.'

'What?'

'I'm going to look simply *awful* in the morning.'

After good nights had been wearily exchanged, Laura replaced the receiver and reached for a bottle of cologne. '*But someone was in the kitchen with you.*' Who was he trying to kid, she thought, re-examining as much as she could recall of Fuller's newest theory. Talk about your sins of omission. I know damn well who he thinks Arthur might have found in the kitchen with me. *Fiona.* Why didn't he come right out with it. More curious, why did I refrain from suggesting it myself?

She unscrewed the bottle cap, sprinkled a few drops of cologne into the palm of her hand and vigorously massaged the back of her neck.

*'Or even worse . . . was Fiona murdered?'*

If so and not by me, by whom and why and where's the body? Added if so, where's her red Volvo? How was the car disposed of? There's been no mention of any sign of it at the cottage when Arthur found me. I'll never sleep now. She sprinkled more cologne and went to work on her wrists.

*'I think Arthur will break. That's your job.'*

You're not all that perceptive, Clive Fuller. Arthur's already been broken. The man you see today is the result of the pieces haphazardly stitched together like a patchwork quilt. His mother caused the first fissures years ago, the sound of shattering humanity was heard sometime after our marriage. Arthur has been a failure with everything but his business. It's all he's got. Probably without it he just might as well be dead. Now I'm feeling sorry for you, Arthur, and that better be a step in the right direction.

She drew up her knees as a chin rest with her hands clasped around them and further pursued the enigmatic husband. She decided to begin at the beginning.

Eight years ago I meet you, somehow there's a mutual attraction and we marry. I must have done my damnedest to make the marriage work. But instead of changing you, I changed myself. You must have been very possessive, Arthur, and this much I have come to remember about myself, I cannot be totally possessed. I will share, but I will not capitulate. You must have been possessive of me because I was all you had. I resisted and you lost me. I blossomed, you withered. Nothing to cling to but your business, your position in life. What a terrible loneliness you suffer. Then perhaps Fiona is in London and you meet

148

her by chance. You're drawn to each other. There's new hope. You're a man again. You might think this is the last time it will ever happen and you make up your mind not to lose it. For mutually agreed reasons, the affair is kept clandestine. Perhaps eventual marriage is discussed, but each has a bond to break before that can be realised. Arthur with Laura, Fiona with Auriol.

Laura rolled over on her stomach and continued thinking.

Meantime, I supposedly plunge myself into a hedonistic whirl in Harborford as undoubtedly reported to Arthur by Fiona. Sean Coleridge, Edmund Kettering, Frank Welbeck, take your pick, any one will serve its purpose. . . . The time is now right for Arthur to ask for a divorce, and for Fiona to sever the cord that binds her to Auriol. Fiona makes the first move (I am assuming) and has a knockdown dragout with Auriol, but doesn't flee directly to Arthur, she comes to *me*.

Laura raised her head.

*Fiona trusted me. I must* have known about Fiona and Arthur! And *approved*. She must have received the threatening note sometime that *Sunday*.

Laura sat up.

Does Auriol know about the note? No, or she would have said something after Fiona disappeared. Think hard, Laura, think hard, there's no sleeping tonight so you might just as well think hard. What would Auriol and Fiona fight about other then the housekeeping expenses? A man most likely. Auriol suspects Coleridge, Kettering or Welbeck and is having none of any of them. There were undoubtedly words from Fiona about Auriol and Welbeck. Maybe Auriol bops her one. I wouldn't put that past Auriol, not after what Brian Cummings went through tonight. Of course! To Auriol, Fiona's defection is legitimate. That's why she hasn't turned her over to missing persons. Now back to the threatening note. What kind of nut sends a note like that without realising he or she can soon be traced in a circle as small and tightly knit as ours is in Harborford?

Laura realised she was shivering and drew the blanket up to her neck.

*What kind of nut?* A jealous nut. Someone blindly terrified of losing a person they think they possess. Now who is our most likely candidate?

Slowly, the blanket slid from her shoulders. Her palms felt sweaty and her mouth was dry. Like a somnambulist, she left the bed for the bathroom, drew a glass of water and sipped it slowly, staring at herself in the cabinet mirror over the basin.

'I think I know the nut!' she told her reflection. She placed the glass on the basin edge and pointed a finger at the mirror. 'You just may have the answer, you deductively clever Laura Denning! All you have to do is *prove it*!' Her stomach leapt and she retrieved the glass of water and drained it. She hurried back to bed and snuggled under the blanket feeling very satisfied with herself. There were still loose ends to be tied together, she reminded herself, but us Girl Scouts know how to tie a knot or two!

Us Girl Scouts? Eureka! I remember! I was a Girl Scout! And so what, unless I'm thinking of pinning this on Baden-Powell and he's been dead for years.

She busied herself with pencil and notebook. She recorded every suspicion and supposition and then re-read them carefully. She looked up and plunged into thought again. Clive Fuller admits he can be wrong and I must try to be equally modest. This can be wrong, all wrong, but it reads too well not to pursue it. But with care, with gentle, devious care, and by myself.

By myself.

She reached for the bottle of cologne, unscrewed the cap and dampened her palm. She rubbed the liquid gently on her throat. It was cool and invigorating with a subtle aroma unlike the deadly sweetness of heliotrope.

Heliotrope.

She lowered her hand.

150

Fiona. Heliotrope. Arthur. Oh, how I shall win Arthur! She snapped her fingers, riffled the notebook to a page containing Elaine Murdock's home number, consulted her wristwatch and, after a brief struggle with her conscience, decided to wait until morning.

She would greet Arthur in the morning with a warm, cheerful hello. She would put her arm through his and together cross the tarmac to the helicopter. She would ask Arthur if he had slept well, and if he hadn't, make appropriate sympathetic noises. When they arrived in Harborford, she would ask Arthur to take her on a tour of the cottage. And after lunch she would ask Arthur to take her for a private walk along the cliff.

But it was important to her she greet Arthur at the airport with the scent of heliotrope.

## Chapter Thirteen

It was almost one a.m. when Sean Coleridge and Edmund Kettering left the Grace and Favour together. Though the Doctor had an early surgery the next morning, he accepted Coleridge's invitation for a nightcap aboard the *Atlantis*. The sky was starless and black and the damp air hung heavily over their damp spirits. They could hear the water lapping against the pilings and Coleridge thought the wharf was swaying, or had he had too much to drink? The moon appeared briefly from behind a cloud like an inquisitive neighbour at a window, and then disappeared again when they reached the boat.

In Sean's claustrophobic cabin, when each man holding a tumbler of scotch sat across from each other on opposing bunks, Coleridge broke the silence. 'They're policemen.' Kettering nodded and drank. He could still hear Laura's name spoken by Aubrey Lewis, still see Brian's elbow con-

151

necting with Aubrey's lower rib, and still harboured the inexplicable fear that overtook him then.

'Come on, Ed. What's it all about?'

'I don't know,' said the Doctor, and he drank again.

'You were there!' persisted Coleridge. 'You were at the cottage that day! It wasn't any bloody prowler. It was nothing like that at all, else why the police?'

Kettering looked up slowly as he spoke. 'I don't know and that's the honest truth.'

'You know,' said Coleridge grimly, 'but you've been told to keep your mouth shut.'

'That's it, and let it lie there.'

'But Laura's in trouble. I *love* her.'

'I can't help you there either.'

'Has it something to do with Fiona's disappearance?'

'I don't *know*, damn it!' He held the glass between his legs and stared into it. 'I don't know.'

Coleridge moved to the porthole and in the glass could see the Doctor's reflection, still staring into the tumbler of scotch, and slowly shaking his head back and forth like a horse trying to free itself from a restraining fetter. Coleridge turned and stared at him. 'What's troubling you, Ed?' he asked.

Kettering looked up and Coleridge was shocked to see the Doctor's eyes brimming with tears.

'Jesus, Ed,' said Coleridge, taking a step forward awkwardly, 'I know how you feel about Laura too, but . . .'

'Do you *really*?' Kettering's voice was an unsuspected volume. 'Do you really know, Sean? You don't, mate, you positively don't.' He placed the tumbler on the table and wiped his eyes with a jacket sleeve. Coleridge could barely hear the Doctor when he spoke again. 'I'm ashamed of what I've been thinking, but it's there and it's got to come out.' His voice rose again. 'I was thinking of Laura and Viola on this boat. I was thinking of that day we hit the squall and Viola went overboard. And God help me, why do I keep asking myself . . . did she really fall? *Was it really an accident?*'

Coleridge went white. The Doctor lunged to his feet and ran from the cabin. Immobile, Coleridge could hear him clambering to the deck, heard his running footsteps down the gangplank on to the wharf, resisted an urge to pursue and throttle him, and with that thought flung his tumbler of scotch against the wall and stood staring at the shattered glass on the floor, unable to control his trembling hands.

The next morning, Elaine Murdock instructed the chauffeur to wait for her outside a Bond Street boutique. It took her a short time to complete the purchase assigned her earlier by phone by Laura Denning, and five minutes later the police car was nosing its way through traffic to Dr Flint's sanatorium.

Laura waited patiently in her room, packed suitcase resting near the door. She had shared coffee and toast with the Doctor who seemed assured she was fit to undertake the trip to Harborford. He told her she looked amazingly fresh and youthful, and Laura silently blessed Elizabeth Arden. She and she alone knew the amount of make-up it took to camouflage the trenches the sleepless night had left beneath her eyes. Dr Flint cautioned that rest was essential (but not for us wicked, thought Laura), and if there was any danger sign of a relapse, Edmund Kettering would receive full instructions from him later in the morning about medication. He wished her luck as Elaine Murdock arrived to announce the car was waiting.

Ten minutes later in the back seat of the police car, Laura eagerly unwrapped the package proferred by Elaine, generously dabbed herself with the heliotrope scent, and offered a silent prayer that Arthur hadn't caught a cold overnight and was in complete possession of his sense of smell. Operation perfume completed, she settled back in the seat and wondered aloud if Fuller had apprised Elaine of Brian Cummings' serio-comic encounter with Auriol Kendall the previous evening. Elaine said he hadn't so

153

Laura did. Elaine laughed and then worried about her husband's facial bruises. Laura took her mind off that by repeating most of her phone conversation with Fuller concerning Arthur's possible position in the case. Elaine absorbed the information like a blotting pad but made no comment.

Before leaving his flat for the airport, Clive Fuller phoned Arthur Denning to offer him a lift. When there was no reply he considered trying him at his office where he might have gone to leave last minute instructions for his staff, but after a quick glance at his wristwatch realised he himself would be late if he didn't get a move on.

At the airport, the two women were met by the helicopter pilot who led them to a private waiting room. There was no sign of either Fuller or Arthur and Laura glanced at her wristwatch. As she looked up, Clive Fuller hurried into the room, a suitcase in one hand, a briefcase in the other, muttering excuses and oaths about morning traffic. The look of welcome on Laura's face was a greeting in itself and the pilot told them the winds were favourable. Fuller motioned Laura to a seat next to him and then unzipped the briefcase, extracted a small folder and asked her to study the photographs it contained.

Laura recognised Frank Welbeck immediately, associating the photo with one she undoubtedly saw in the past in a newspaper or magazine. Fuller told her the picture had probably been taken five years ago when the project now occupying him was first announced. 'The lines in his face are deeper and his hair is greyer,' Fuller told Laura.

The next photograph bore a marked resemblance to Welbeck and Laura recognised the woman as probably Emaline. 'She does look like a hawk,' commented Laura. 'When was it taken?'

'Same day as Welbeck's. The face is thinner today and the features more pronounced. She and her brother are quite tall, almost the same height.'

Fuller handed her a newspaper clipping headed 'Corn-

154

wall Tragedy'. There was a candid photograph identified as Dr Edmund Kettering. He was obviously caught unawares and was staring with astonishment, the mouth about to cry out something. Under the photograph was a brief story about Viola Kettering's death. Laura scanned the sentences and then concentrated on Kettering's face again. 'I seem to know the face,' said Laura. 'I know this one too.' She was holding what looked like a passport photo. 'It's Sean Coleridge, isn't it.'

'His identification photo when he was in the merchant marine. He's ten years older now, but in looks he hasn't aged much.'

'Time is much kinder to men,' Laura stated flatly, and wondered if Fuller was deceived by the heavy make-up under her eyes. Elaine Murdock joined them and busied herself memorising the faces.

Fuller looked at the wall clock and said, 'What the hell's keeping Denning?' He turned to Laura, 'Get any sleep?'

'Not much,' she said.

'It doesn't show.' Her pleasure did. She was almost tempted to share her theory as to who Arthur must have encountered in the kitchen but Fuller began talking again. 'No photos of Auriol Kendall or Fiona Cooper. But undoubtedly you have a fairly accurate mental picture of both by now.' While he spoke, he kept glancing at the wall clock. The pilot was sprawled in an easy chair puffing a cigarette like a steam engine and was obviously as anxious to get underway. It was fifteen minutes past the planned hour of departure.

Nurse Murdock spoke up cheerfully. 'Perhaps he stopped en route to say goodbye to his mother.'

'She said her goodbye years ago,' stated Laura, too late to bite her tongue.

Fuller, briefly engrossed in his own thoughts, didn't hear what she said. He was almost tempted to share with Laura his theory as to who must have sent Fiona the threatening note when the door opened and a tired, haggard Arthur

155

Denning entered carrying a large valise. He packed this morning and in a hurry, deduced Laura, a bit of what looks like a shirt-tail's protruding from the valise. She studied his face, and decided with some surprise he was suffering from a hangover.

'Good morning, Arthur!' she chirped affectionately and then thought the least Fuller could do was pat her on the head. His hand was engaged shaking Arthur's. Arthur managed a weak smile for Laura and the pilot was on his feet suggesting they depart immediately. He led them out the door to the tarmac while Laura positioned herself next to Arthur and locked arms with her astonished husband.

'You're unusually chipper this morning,' Arthur told Laura.

'I feel reborn,' she said gaily while behind her Fuller winced.

The helicopter blades were whirling and Fuller said loudly, 'Duck everyone, let's not lose our heads!' Laura took the remark personally and over her shoulder made a face.

When they were comfortably settled in the vehicle with seat belts strapped, Laura patted Arthur's hand gently and shouted over the engine's roar, 'This is all too exciting! Aren't you excited?' Arthur looked shrivelled. Laura turned her head and smiled at Fuller and Elaine. Fuller was staring out the window at the disappearing ground and a white-faced Nurse Murdock was clutching a silver cross suspended from her neck. Laura turned to Arthur. There was a hand over his mouth and his eyes were closed and she hoped if he was going to be sick he'd have the courtesy to be sick in the opposite direction. She averted her gaze to the pilot. He was chewing gum. She felt secure.

Only three members of the fishing party sailed with the *Atlantis* that morning. Brian Cummings feigned illness and Aubrey Lewis elected to remain with him. When the ship was a speck on the horizon, Brian effected a rapid recovery

156

and he and Aubrey set out to explore the shoreline. At Fuller's suggestion, they were to look for hidden coves and inlets, investigate several caves under the cliffs, whose origins were attributed to yesteryear's pirates and smugglers once based in the territory. They carried hampers of picnic lunch and bottled beer. Aubrey Lewis sang *Yo ho ho and a bottle of rum* while Brian Cummings fingered the welts on his cheek and looked grim.

With a cigarette hanging limply from pursed lips and two boiled sweets shaking in her left hand like a pair of dice, Auriol Kendall stared at the photograph of herself and Fiona and filled with resolve. Two fingers removed the cigarette, the lips parted like a smelting furnace and the sweets were consigned to their fate. She swept from sitting room to kitchen, found a yellow basket and a pair of shears, emerged into the field behind her house and attacked a rose bush with the relish of a crusader slaughtering a Saracen.

An old-age pensioner sat trembling on a chair in Edmund Kettering's surgery, his worn jacket draped over his quivering left hand, his right sleeve rolled up over the elbow. Dr Kettering advanced on him with a hyperdermic syringe tightly held in his right hand. His face was grey and his eyes were dark, puffy slits. The pensioner's heart skipped more beats than a school orchestra. 'This won't hurt a bit,' was Kettering's hollow-sounding promise as he prodded for and found a vein.

'Yoicks!' squealed the old man as the needle found its mark, and had Edmund Kettering been able to see his reflection in a mirror at that moment he might have been shocked by his look of sadistic pleasure.

Emaline Welbeck's kitchen reverberated with blows and thumps as she mercilessly pounded some dough on the kitchen table. She sprinkled the dough with flour and then plunged her fingers into it with the intensity of a strangler attacking a throat. She kneaded and twisted and shaped as though emulating her brother when working in clay. Then satisfied by the feel of the texture, she picked up a knife

157

and plunged it into the mound, severing and dismembering until there were twelve equal portions for the buttered biscuit tin. While wiping her fingers on her soiled apron, she crossed to a window and stared out into the grey morning at her brother's studio. But she could not see in and could only guess at what might be going on in her brother's sanctuary.

In the studio, Frank Welbeck was working on Charlotte Corday's face. He was breathing heavily and oblivious to a lock of hair partially obscuring the vision of his right eye. He worked as though he didn't need his eyes, as though he was transferring a vision in his memory to his fingers. Slowly and with effort as the morning wore on, the face took on a semblance of Laura Denning. It was not quite right and Welbeck feared it would never be quite right, but he persevered.

Aboard the *Atlantis*, Sean Coleridge bellowed orders at his crew like a Captain Ahab sensing the immediate appearance of the mystical white whale. He punctuated commands with streams of tobacco juice over his shoulder into the choppy sea and once misjudged the wind resulting in his face looking like an amateur actor badly made-up for Othello. Billy Merkle, his first mate, was perplexed by his usually placid captain's sudden change of character and attributed it to a rare hangover. Every so often Coleridge peered at the sky, silently hoping for a hint of storm which would give him a logical excuse to order the ship back to port. Amiable questions from his fishing party brought rude grunts or brusque retorts and all were tacitly pleased at the realisation that Aubrey Lewis's rehearsed blunder of the previous evening at the inn had undoubtedly brought about this abrupt change in personality. They hoped their fish would be as easily hooked.

Shortly after noon the helicopter was circling Harborford, and with Arthur Denning's help the pilot sighted a level area adjoining Laura's cottage and began his descent. When Laura stared out the window at the village below, she became filled with a curious and then tingling sensation of *deja vu. I have been here before. I recognise the church. I have strolled across the village square.* Her face was pressed against a window like a small girl outside a sweet-shop. *That should be the inn with the wooden walk leading to the pier.* Fuller was watching her and from the expression on her face perceived what was going on in her mind. Though his heart was rarely given to singing, at the moment, had he been asked, he might have admitted to a muffled trill or two. Their eyes met and there was no need for Laura to speak. Fuller's face was beaming and she knew he understood. She turned to Arthur and shouted in his ear, 'It's coming back to me.' Arthur mouthed 'Bravo' without enthusiasm.

Vicar Owen Farquhar stood on the steps of the church staring at the descending helicopter. He began bouncing like a desperate man standing in a queue at a public lavatory and brought his hands together in a thunderous clap, inadvertently killing a mosquito.

Villagers strolling or sunning themselves in the square shaded their eyes as they watched the descending helicopter. Realisation began to dawn and word began to spread that Laura Denning has come home.

Auriol Kendall stood behind her house adjusting her field glasses. They served her well as they had served her husband in India. She brought the pilot into focus then moved the glasses slightly and found Laura. She felt as though she could reach out and print her name for Laura on the window. Somehow seeing Laura again brought her closer to the missing Fiona. Her lips began trembling, her eyes began misting and she lowered the glasses. She felt blanketed with a strange foreboding and wondered if all her life she had been a fool.

Edmund Kettering leaned out of an open window with hands on the sill bracing his body. He squinted at the sky and saw the helicopter lowering itself towards the ground. He turned back into the room and stared at the wedding photograph of himself and Viola. His stomach felt constricted and he crossed to his surgery where he mixed himself a large bicarbonate of soda.

Emaline Welbeck was pacing in a circle in front of the door to the studio like an alien lioness waiting to be invited to join the pack. Frank Welbeck was at a window on the opposite side watching the helicopter disappear behind a line of trees that bordered Laura's property. 'It's them!' he heard his sister growl. 'I'm baking her favourite biscuits! I'm going to take them straight over and welcome her home! Amnesia or no amnesia, she'll remember my biscuits!' Frank loped across the studio floor and flung open the door.

'You'll stay right here till you're invited over there!'

'Oh, Frankie!' she cried elatedly with arms outstretched, 'you're talking to me! Oh, Frankie, Frankie! You forgive your Emaline!'

'*My* Emaline,' he mimicked her viciously, 'makes me want to puke!'

'Oh, anything you say, Frankie! Anything! Laura's back and Arthur's back and everything's going to be just fine!'

'Oh yes, Emaline. Oh yes, indeed. Everything's going to be just great. Everything's going to be just the way Emaline wants it.'

She clapped her hands gleefully.

'And your biscuits are going to be just fine too, Emaline. Just the way Laura likes them.' He was pointing towards the kitchen. Her head darted around and she saw wisps of smoke drifting from the open door.

'My biscuits!' she screeched, 'my biscuits!' She raised her skirts and leapt towards the kitchen. Welbeck threw back his head and roared with laughter and then just as abruptly it strangled in his throat. He realised he hadn't laughed in over a month.

Chewing ferociously on a cud of tobacco, Sean Coleridge gripped the deck rail and his eyes scanned the coast line as he thought, *She must be back by now, she must be.*

160

On his right, two of the fishing party had their lines cast in the sea, while one chattered on aimlessly about a romantic conquest in the wilds of Hampstead Heath. The other abruptly gripped his pole and shouted, 'Save it for later! I've got a bite!' and Coleridge rushed to his cabin and poured himself a large scotch.

'Don't look down! *Don't look down!*

Through perspiration dripping from his eyelids, Brian Cummings stared at the whites of Aubrey Lewis's knuckles. Aubrey had a powerful grip on Brian's right wrist. Brian raised his eyes with an effort and saw every muscle and vein straining in Aubrey's neck and chin. Aubrey gasped, 'There's a rock jutting out near your right foot. Try to get a balance on it!'

Brian was swaying against the cliff face. He moved his foot an inch, desperately hoping to make immediate contact with the jutting rock.

'More to the right!' gasped Aubrey, 'another couple of inches!'

So long, Elaine. I hope you know how much I've loved you. Try to understand I never meant to fall off this cliff. The ground under my feet seemed safe enough when I was looking over the edge. You know Aubrey is like an Indian guide. He saw these dried up traces of oil and said they probably dripped from some car, and what would a car be doing out in this wasteland? And so we came to the edge of the cliff, and Aubrey warned me not to get too close and I was yelling it's as solid as the Common Market which must have been prophetic because that's when the ground gave way under me and I started to go over and Aubrey lunged forward and made a grab for my jacket and caught my wrist instead and here I am swinging back and forth like some ruddy pendulum on a grandfather's clock and where's that bleeding rock his hand is sweaty and beginning to slip . . .

'You're there,' gasped Aubrey from the bottom of his throat.

Brian felt the rock through the sole of his shoe, wedged his foot on to it and luckily it held. He pressed against the cliff face with a silent prayer on his lips as Aubrey twisted his body and brought his left hand down and took a firm grip on Brian's lower arm.

'Ready?' shouted Aubrey.

'Yuh,' Brian managed to respond.

Aubrey inhaled deeply and with one powerful heave brought Brian up to a point where his stomach met the cliff edge. Aubrey swiftly released one hand and clutched at Brian's trouser seat. He inhaled again and with another powerful heave brought Brian to safety. Aubrey sat on the ground panting heavily. Brian remained face downward and unseen by Aubrey, kissed the earth beneath his face.

'Well, old cock,' said Aubrey when he was breathing normally again, 'thought we were seeing the last of you then.'

Brian pushed himself up to a sitting position and shoved his nose against Aubrey's. 'Not a word of this to Fuller or the wife, or I'll do you!'

'Not a word,' echoed Aubrey as he gingerly peered over the edge of the cliff where the waves were pounding at a circle of jagged rocks in a cove obviously worn away by centuries of erosion. The rocks now formed the perimeter of a natural pool and through the rapidly ebbing tide, Aubrey commented he could see a distant reflection of Brian's bright red hair.

'Don't be daft,' said the exhausted Brian who was sitting at least five feet away from the edge feeling cold and sick.

'I'm not daft,' said Aubrey evenly, lying on his stomach with his face hanging over the edge, 'I see a tiny red dot under the water.' Brian bravely inched his way to Aubrey's side and stared down into the pool. He fought a rising dizziness at the sight of the long drop he had almost taken.

162

'Oh my Gawd,' he said in a voice like a bow drawn across untuned strings.

Aubrey chuckled. 'They'd have had to sew you together mate, you know.'

'Oh my Gawd,' repeated Brian, struggling to retain his lunch. He rolled over on his back and sat up with an effort. After swallowing several times, he was able to speak. 'Have to look for a path.'

Aubrey rolled over on his side and stared at his friend inquisitively. 'What ever for?'

'Have to get down there somehow . . . for a closer look.'

'What *at*?'

'The bloody blob of red, you nit.' Brian turned and their eyes locked. 'Bloody blob of red like in red Volvo.'

Chapter Fourteen

'It's Royalties!' shouted Laura triumphantly as Arthur assisted her from the helicopter. 'Of course it's my cottage!' She took several steps forward as Fuller and Elaine Murdock alighted behind her. 'My wisteria's blooming! And look at how the lilac bush in the doorway is blooming! I planted it *myself*!' She clasped her hands and ran forward as though to greet the shade of Walt Whitman.

'I knew it!' said Elaine Murdock, trotting alongside Fuller after her knee painfully connected with his swinging suitcase, 'I knew it would start coming back to her once we got her here . . . *ouch*!' The suitcase had connected again and Fuller apologised. He had been concentrating on Arthur's face which he found a perplexing study. It was totally blank, like a freshly whitewashed wall cautioning *Post No Bills*. He had earlier picked up Arthur's suitcase and found it unusually light, as though he had only planned an overnight stay. He had barely spoken five sentences

163

throughout the trip, and Laura's determined efforts to show affection to him were met with passive resistance. Fuller's emotions as he followed Laura were a mixture of a strange uneasiness about Arthur and an inner elation of Laura's steady reawakening.

Behind the four the helicopter was slowly returning to the sky and Elaine Murdock decided the least she could do was to wave her arm in farewell to the pilot who had safely deposited them. Laura was studying the welcome mat at the side door as though it was a piece in a puzzle. She knelt, lifted the mat, felt around and was rewarded. She jumped to her feet and held the metal object high for all to see.

'The spare key! The spare key I *always* leave under the mat because I'm always forgetting *mine*! How's *that*, Mr Fuller?'

'Does it fit the lock?' he inquired in mock logic.

Laura grabbed the doorknob as she aimed the key at the lock and the door swung open. 'Point killer,' she murmured as over her shoulder she shouted, 'Some damn fool's left the door unlocked!' She entered the sitting room.

Measured steps brought her to the centre of the room and slowly she turned, absorbing every item it contained as though it were on display at the National Gallery. *I have been here before.* Fuller was the next to enter the room and Laura said to him, 'My study is through that door.'

He put his suitcase down and walked to the door she was indicating. She spoke again as he approached it, 'My desk is near the window overlooking the sea. My typewriter's on that desk and there's probably a half-typed page of manuscript still in it, unless you've removed it when you were last here.'

'No,' said Fuller, the door now ajar, 'I read it, but I didn't remove it. Can you recall what you were writing?'

A shiver ran through her as she said without first having to think, 'A physical description of Belle Crippen.' Fuller crossed to the desk, leaned over the typewriter and scanned the description of Belle Crippen.

164

'Score another.' Laura had entered the room while he read.

'Clive.' He turned to her. 'Suddenly I'm frightened. My head's throbbing but not with an ache. I can describe the entire house to you. Did you know this might happen? Did Dr Flint give you any indication?'

'Some, and a psychiatrist friend who works with the Yard.' He told her about his visit with Herkimer the previous day while Elaine Murdock busied herself exploring the upstairs bedrooms. Arthur sat in the living room in a chair facing the couch, applying a match to a cigarette, looking like an unwelcome guest. He was within hearing distance of Laura and Fuller.

Laura let Fuller speak without interruption. She sat at the desk with her arms folded, listening with complete concentration. When he had finished, she said without looking at him, 'Now I'm going into the kitchen.'

Edmund Kettering latched the door to his surgery from the inside and then poured himself a brandy. For the past hour during ten hasty examinations and eight hastily scrawled prescriptions, he'd begun to feel a fool. He began to feel his outburst in Coleridge's cabin before his dramatic exit was unfair and uncalled for. Unfair to Laura whom he professed to love and uncalled for in front of Coleridge who would be smart enough to conclude the outburst was an accusation of murder. He downed the brandy and refilled the glass. It was five hours since Dr Flint had phoned him the precautionary medication. It was four hours since he had driven to the cottage with a carton of groceries and neatly placed them in larder and refrigerator. It was only now he remembered the time spent in the kitchen had so unnerved him, he had replaced the key under the mat without locking the side door. He shrugged it away and returned to Sean Coleridge.

What a bloody fool I was behaving the way I did last night. Coleridge is no intellectual, but he's no idiot. Like everyone else in the village he suspects there's a deeper significance to the detective returning here with Laura. I hinted at murder last night and he's bound to have added it up by now. Must I tell this to Fuller? If I do, I have to repeat what I said about Laura and Viola. He stared at a wall. There was no hole for him to crawl into.

What did I actually say? I wasn't all that tight. Tight enough, but not all that tight. The hell with it. The ruddy bloody hell with it. He downed the brandy. I'll tell Fuller what little I remember. He's had weeks in which to formulate some theories of his own about what happened to Laura in the cottage. Flint's positive her memory block will soon begin to crumble. There have been healthy signs of it in London. For all I know, she's recalled it all by now.

Christ! Christ! Is Fiona mixed up in this in any way? Should I have told Fuller *what I know about Fiona*?

'The bloodstains were here,' said Fuller, indicating the wall next to the stove, 'and there was a pool of blood near the kitchen table, as a matter of fact, just about where you're standing.'

Laura held her ground and stared at the floor. 'And on the kitchen table, right?' she asked clinically. Fuller nodded. Laura walked to the kitchen door, opened it and surveyed the fieldstone path that led to the edge of the cliff. 'And not a trace of any on the path?'

'None.'

She remained standing in the doorway. 'Was there a blanket on the bed Fiona presumably slept in?'

'There was.'

She retraced her steps to the kitchen table. 'Clive, I had a char. I know I did.' She rubbed a finger against her cheek and stared unseeing at the ceiling. 'Strange little thing. Never said much and never cleaned much either for that fact.'

'Gertrude Clay,' said Fuller, 'you gave her the sack about two months ago. She apparently disturbed your desk con-

166

trary to orders and you threw her out of the house, to quote Mrs Clay.'

'Well I trust it didn't jar *her* memory,' she said with hands on hips. 'She'd know the contents of the linen closet and if any blankets were missing.'

'She knew the contents and nothing was missing.'

'And undoubtedly started all the gossip in the village.'

'Oh, yes,' said Fuller archly, 'the village is whispering dark deeds. There hasn't been so much gossip, the constables tell me, since Viola Kettering fell overboard.'

Laura's eyebrows shot up. 'Almost forgot about that.' She was examining the contents of the refrigerator. 'Well, if that *wasn't* an accident, do you suppose it has some connection with this kitchen?'

'Perhaps. You were there too.'

'Thank you for your vote of confidence. Somebody's filled the fridge.'

'And the larder. Dr Kettering. I asked Dr Flint to tell him to get some food in when he phoned him this morning.' Laura shot him an inquisitive look. 'In case you need medication. Relapse. All that.'

'Oh, yes. Forgot.' She slammed the refrigerator door shut and crossed to the larder. 'Tinned soups. I *loathe* tinned soups. Ed knows better than that.'

'Does he?' The pipe stem was in his mouth.

'I said it, didn't I?' she stated firmly. 'I'm hungry. I'll do lunch.' She reached for a loaf of bread and crossed with it to the table, on the way removing a bread board from a hook on the wall. At the table, she opened a drawer, reached in and picked up a carving knife. She placed the knife on the table, crossed back to the refrigerator, reached for the handle, thought for a quick moment, and her hand froze. She moved her head slowly until her eyes were in a direct line to the carving knife. It was pearl-handled. 'When did you find time to put it there?'

'Brian brought it with him. Arthur told us about the key under the mat. We have our own set which I was holding on to in case you didn't remember where the key was.'

'It *is* the knife, isn't it?'

'Yes.'

'Pretty.' She crossed to the knife and picked it up. She examined it carefully and again felt its weight. 'It's not my knife.'

'You're sure?'

'It's not my knife.' She opened the drawer again. 'Come over here and see for yourself.' He joined her at the drawer. 'Everything in this drawer is a matched set. It's Danish. I bought it in Copenhagen.'

'When?'

'About five years ago. There was a Writer's Congress and I was a delegate. I remember distinctly the fuss I had with customs when I returned and . . .'

'Don't stop,' he said sharply.

'Wait a minute! Wait a minute!' She studied the knife again. 'I've seen this knife or one like it *before*.'

They didn't hear Arthur Denning leave the house.


Brian Cummings and Aubrey Lewis finally found a path that led to the hidden cove. About a hundred yards from the site of Brian's accident, the escarpment curved inward. There, roughly hewn steps had been cut into the cliff face.

'Looks like they haven't been used in years,' commented Brian.

Said Aubrey eagerly, 'Bet pirates cut them hundreds of years ago! Better let me go first.'

Brian didn't argue. They made their way down slowly and cautiously and on Brian's nervous part, reluctantly. But there might be treasure ahead for them too, and that thought spurred him on. A little red treasure.


'*Think!*' Fuller urged Laura who was sitting at the kitchen table staring at the pearl-handled carving knife.

'I *am* thinking but I can't remember whose house! But it belongs to somebody I know. I'm *positive* of that. Somebody who lives here in Harborford.' She slammed her fist on the table. 'Why don't we make the rounds with it?'

'And give the game away?'

'Why in hell not?' asked Laura hotly. 'What are we pussyfooting around for?' She was out of the chair and pacing back and forth. 'What's the point in shrouding ... no pun intended ... the truth? Those notes you had me dictate to Arthur have undoubtedly had their effect. Do you still think I might be the guilty party?'

'No.' The word nestled in her ear like a contented puppy.

'Then let's bring the facts out in the open! Dear friends! A murder has been committed! We know one of you is guilty! Now talk up so the rest of us can get on with our lives!'

'How do we know one of them is guilty?' he inquired slyly. 'It could be some total stranger, or are you hiding a fresh theory from me?'

'I wasn't deliberately holding out on you,' she said with an innocence he immediately discounted. 'I wanted to meet and talk with this person before cementing my suspicion.' She spoke the name. 'Now you'll tell me it's at the top of your list.'

'And heavily underlined.'

'Two great minds,' she said dully as she sat again, right elbow on table and chin propped in the palm of the hand.

Fuller had sliced some bread and was buttering it like a barber honing a straight-blade razor. 'We just can't walk up to our pigeon and say here you, we know you're guilty now out with it, why and where's the body. It's not that simple.' He bit into the bread and spoke as he chewed. 'I could suggest attempting to drive our pigeon around the bend, but I think they've been in residence there for years.'

Laura had crossed to the sitting room entrance to assure herself the room was empty and then accepted a slice of bread and butter. They could hear bustling about in the room above. 'Arthur doesn't look too good,' she said and Fuller agreed with her diagnosis. 'Somehow that makes me feel we're getting very close to wrapping this up. I'm almost positive he's convinced the person he met in the kitchen is the murderer. I don't think he's realised this until just the past few days.'

'Why so?'

'Because I think he's been suspecting it's Fiona. But I don't think he's heard from her and if Fiona was on the lam, she'd need help and Arthur would be the logical person for her to turn to, *if* they're really all that involved, and I think they are. Of course by the process of elimination . . .'

Her slice of bread was down to the crust and she was staring at it as though she had found a concealed message. Fuller was wiping his fingers on a paper napkin, knowing full well that when she spoke, she would name the victim.

'Fiona.'

'That's right. It could only be Fiona who's been murdered.'

Auriol Kendall screamed. She had been standing in the open kitchen doorway unheard and unseen by the others, arms laden with flowers. Laura and Fuller rushed to her as she began to pitch forward, the flowers spilling from her hands. They helped the moaning woman to a chair as Fuller wondered whether to call for smelling salts or a boiled sweet. Nurse Murdock came tearing into the room and shouted, 'I heard a scream!'

'Smelling salts,' said Fuller, and Nurse Murdock shot back into the sitting room for her first aid kit.

Eyes open though glazed, Auriol's head fell back. 'The beast,' she said in a strangled voice, 'the foul beast . . . if he had known the truth . . . if I had only told him the truth . . .'

Edmund Kettering entered through the kitchen door, and Laura was the first to espy him. 'Well, just don't stand there, Eddie,' she said sharply, 'Auriol needs help. She's had a shock! Oh!' A look of astonished delight was on her face. 'Well it *is* Ed Kettering, isn't it?'

'You remember me,' he said gratefully, like a retired actress recognised in a crowd.

'Why, Eddie,' said Laura coyly, 'how could I ever forget *you*!' Nurse Murdock was back with the smelling salts and waving them under Auriol's nose. The Doctor joined them and felt for Auriol's pulse.

'Beast . . . beast . . . you've murdered your daughter. . . .'

Frank Welbeck was carefully buffing Charlotte Corday's face. From the moment Emaline went to the rescue of her burning biscuits, a sudden inspiration overtook and empowered him. He tightly bolted the studio door, studied the statue and went to work. The minutes flew as he fashioned the features into the resemblance that had been eluding him. But now it was right. It was what it should have been but he couldn't bring himself to do.

When he was satisfied, he stepped back and surveyed the finished product with pride.

'Perfect!' he shouted at the lifeless form, 'absolutely perfect! Better then the first one!'

He wiped his fingers on a soiled towel and then crossed to the window that looked out on the house. He peered towards the kitchen but could detect no sign of Emaline moving about. Cautiously, he unbolted the door, poked his head out, peered about, then stepped forward and bolted the door behind him. Stealthily he made his way to the kitchen door. He could detect the smell of burnt biscuits and on the table he saw the half-charred remains.

'Emaline?' he whispered and then, satisfied, entered the kitchen. He crossed to a door that led to the basement and opened it with caution. He groped for and found the light switch, and the bulb at the foot of the stairs emitted a feeble glow. He descended rapidly, crossed to a rusted foot locker, groped in his pocket for his keys and after pulling back the lid, dug beneath old garments and found a frayed leather box. He opened it, examined the contents and selected an object. He whispered to himself, 'And now for the unkindest cut of all.'

When Arthur left the cottage, he did so with resolve and determination. It was brought about by the conversation he'd been overhearing between Laura and Fuller in the kitchen.

*I've seen this knife or one like it before.*

So have I, Arthur realised, so have I. He strode hastily towards the row of trees that separated Laura's and the Welbeck's property. He emerged in the clearing where the five statues were grouped. He moved past the statues to the house.

In the kitchen, Emaline was mourning the burnt biscuits. Then anger overtook her and she berated them. 'Stupid things! *Now* what do I bring my darling Laura? What what what!' She puzzled the problem in silence and then inspiration clicked in her head. 'That's it! *Sea heath!* She *loves* sea heath!' Emaline opened a closet door, found a basket and a large pair of shears, placed a bonnet on her head, tying the string loosely under her chin, and then skipped across the room and out the door in the direction of the cliffs. Merrily she sang under her breath, '*Maybe it's the moon over Corn ... wallllll. ...*'

Arthur tried the front door of the Welbeck house and it was unlocked. He entered the hall, crossed through the sitting room, past the dining room and into the kitchen. In the kitchen, he saw the tin of burnt biscuits, the cupboard door ajar, the kitchen door open. He crossed to the kitchen door and stared at the studio. As always, the door was shut and the windows were covered. With unflagging resolve, he started for the studio when in the distance he espied what he thought was a familiar figure, bonneted and carrying a basket, heading towards the distant cliffs, towards the hidden cove where once, and it seemed in some long-lost age, he and Laura had strolled romantically on many moonlit nights. He altered his course to that direction.

Brian Cummings and Aubrey Lewis, exhausted but excited, unmindful of the tears in their clothes, their dirt-

172

caked faces and bruised fingers, were rapidly skirting the cliff edge heading towards Laura's cottage. From a distance, they saw but did not recognise Auriol Kendall approaching the kitchen door. Then they heard what was a faint but unmistakable scream, and as they increased their stride to a trot, saw a car pull up at the front of the cottage and a man emerge and walk around the side of the house to the kitchen door.

Sean Coleridge stood immobile at the prow of his ship, his face as settled and blank as Garbo's in the final frames of *Queen Christina*. An overpowering anxiety to see Laura had made him decide to abruptly curtail the trip and bark an order to return to port. There were no cries of surprise, anger or dissent from the three members of the fishing party, and the crew had long been trained never to countermand an order. Sean chartered a return course to run parallel to the cliffside. He wanted to see Royalties and perhaps lift his cap in salute to the goddess back in residence there. For the past hour he'd been suffering an inner struggle, and when the internal enemy had been overcome and subdued with the aid of three neat scotches, he gave his orders, moved to the prow and silently rehearsed the speech he planned to make when he and Laura would be walking alone, arm in arm, along the cliff edge.

The speech, as he now re-rehearsed it in his mind, was one-third Coleridge, one-third films he recalled seeing, and one-third paperbacks he occasionally attempted to read.

'Laura,' it began, 'I've missed you terribly. I know now life is unbearably empty without you. I want you to divorce Arthur and marry me.' Somewhere he thought he heard violins. 'I don't care who you've murdered. I'll stand by you and I know you'll beat this rap. Then let me take you away from all this. My boat's a sturdy craft and we can set sail for the tropics.' Violins gave way to the soft slur of a Hawaiian guitar and for a brief moment Dorothy Lamour in an orchid-print sarong almost obscured the angelic vision of Laura. 'You're all I want in this world and you know I can make you happy. We make it great in the sack. But why am I telling you all this? You know it as well as I do. I'll be a good provider. We'll haul coconut husks and dried fish and trade conch shells and beads with the natives.

'Don't scream, baby . . . I know you never thought you'd ever hear me talking so tenderly. . . .'

The scream blew across the water again and Coleridge realised it came from the direction of the cliff.

*Laura!*

His head spun round and he saw someone on the cliff's edge above the hidden cove with arms flailing. The person appeared to have lost their balance and was falling backwards. The wind delivered the echo of another terrified shriek and to Coleridge's horror shared with the others drawn to the leeward rail, they saw the figure plummet into space.

'Oh my God!' someone shouted.

Sean Coleridge was frozen to the rail.

'I think I heard someone's name!' another voice chorused.

'That was no name,' said Billy Merkle. 'It's the word every poor soul shouts before meeting their Maker.' He turned to the others and solemnly repeated the word, *'Mother.'*

Chapter Fifteen

Vicar Owen Farquhar pulled in at the side of Laura's cottage and parked behind Dr Kettering's car. He opened the door, eased himself out from behind the wheel as though divesting himself of a girdle, and was chagrined to hear the sound of a woman sobbing from the direction of the kitchen. Poor Laura, he thought sadly, the poor lamb is

174

overcome by her return to the fold. He considered the discretion of removing himself and returning later in the day, and swiftly reminded himself that it was he who was ordained to give comfort to others. He clasped his hands in front of him, and with head bowed, walked slowly to the kitchen door which was still ajar.

Approaching in the distance from the opposite direction to the cottage, Brian Cummings with Aubrey Lewis trotting alongside him was the first to see the Vicar with hands clasped and head bowed and wrongly assumed another tragedy had occurred. He poked Aubrey, indicated the Vicar, and they increased their speed.

Auriol Kendall sat on the kitchen chair rocking and keening. The smelling salts had been replaced by a jigger of brandy which she held lightly between thumb and index finger without spilling a drop.

'It's the truth, it's the truth,' she said between heavy sobs, 'Frank Welbeck is Fiona's father.'

There was a demure gasp from the doorway and all eyes turned to the Vicar as he stopped in his tracks. Laura studied the cherub for a few moments and then recognition flooded her face. She stretched her arms out and said, 'Hello, my dearest Owen.' The Vicar's face lit up as he rushed to Laura and they embraced.

'Welcome home,' he said in a choked voice, and then whispered in her ear, 'It's been hell.'

'*Men!*' Auriol shrieked, and the Vicar jumped and clutched Laura tightly. Laura patted his back gently and, with some embarrassment, the Vicar backed away with a shy smile and directed his attention to Auriol.

Nurse Murdock was leaning against the kitchen sink with her arms folded. Dr Kettering was standing with his back to the window staring at Laura. Clive Fuller had positioned himself in front of Auriol.

'Was that what you and Fiona argued about that Sunday night?'

She shook her head violently. 'No! Never! She didn't

175

know! The argument was something else,' she heaved and sobbed and sipped some brandy, 'something equally ... *scandalous*. Oh, what's the use! What's the use! The Vicar knows! Ed knows! The whole world might just as well know! My poor child! My poor Fiona!' She looked up, tears gushing from her eyes. 'Fiona was *pregnant*.'

Laura's hand flew to her mouth and she turned to Ed Kettering who nodded gravely. She crossed the room to Auriol, knelt at her side and put her arms around her. 'There there,' she crooned, 'there there.'

Auriol's head shot up as her face twisted with a vicious sneer. 'There there your uncle! She was pregnant with *her own father's child*!'

The yelp was Nurse Murdock's and Ed Kettering rushed to steady the swaying Vicar.

'She didn't tell you *that*!' snapped Laura angrily.

'Well, she didn't deny it either! I need another brandy!'

Elaine Murdock crossed to the table, picked up the bottle and refilled Auriol's jigger. Laura turned to the Vicar and Dr Kettering. 'You both knew about this. Did she name Frank Welbeck to either of you?'

The Vicar bit his lip as his face reddened and lowered again, his second chin protruding like a blob of inflated bubble gum.

'Well, did she, Ed?'

Dr Kettering looked on the verge of tears and he spoke softly. 'It was Arthur's child.'

The table shook as though an earthquake had struck as Auriol's fist slammed down on it. 'Arthur *Denning*?' she shouted. 'Arthur *Denning*? *Laura's* Arthur Denning?'

'I'm afraid so,' said Laura as she got to her feet, 'not all of Fiona's field trips produced butterflies. Clive, to recoin a cliche, there's no time like the present. Tell them.'

Precisely and without wasting words, Clive Fuller revealed the truth of his presence in Harborford and his and Laura's deduction there was an affair between Arthur and Fiona. Brian Cummings and Aubrey Lewis reached the kitchen door while Fuller was expounding, and Elaine Murdock who was the first to notice them, crossed her lips with an index finger and then mouthed a kiss at Brian who signalled her thumbs up.

Auriol looked at Laura. 'Fiona came here to you that night?'

'Yes,' said Laura. 'She must have admitted the truth to me and that's why I probably phoned Arthur. And by the way, where is *he*?'

'He went out,' said Elaine Murdock. 'I saw him from your bedroom window. I think he was headed for the Welbeck's.'

'Fiona can't be dead! She can't be!' Auriol wailed.

'I'm afraid she is.' All eyes turned to Brian Cummings. He addressed his next remark to Fuller. 'We've found her car. It's submerged in a hidden cove about a mile up the cliffside. The tide was out. That's how we spotted it.' Aubrey coughed and Cummings blushed.

They heard Auriol ease off the chair like an unloading sack of coal. She landed on her knees and with hands interlaced in supplication she beseeched the ceiling, 'I should have told her the truth! I should have told her then Frank was her father! Then she would have told *me* the truth about her and that adulterous wretch.' Her eyes moved to Laura, 'Your husband.'

Laura was about to snap her own comment on Auriol's adultery but the woman was not to be interrupted. 'I should have stayed with her in India!' followed by an intake of breath and Laura saw the breach and plunged into it.

'Then you *were* pregnant *before* you went to India!'

'Yes, yes,' Auriol responded with despair, 'my husband knew the whole story. For a boor and a martinet he was terribly understanding and married me regardless of my girlhood indiscretion.'

'Didn't Frank know?' asked Laura.

'Neither of *them* knew,' Auriol replied with a growl. 'When my husband was bitten by that insect and succumbed, I returned to England and placed Fiona in a convent school. As far as society was concerned, she was my neice. I bought my property here hoping to reawaken Frank's love, but he was already a dried raisin by then, and I dedicated the rest of my life to Fiona . . . and my art!'

Laura was about to console her with the thought she could always drop over to the Welbeck's and look at the statue of Sappho for which Fiona posed and then immediately dismissed it as a bit too frivolous. Fuller was in a quiet conference with Brian and Aubrey. Auriol was staring at the flowers she'd brought for Laura, rescued from the floor by Elaine Murdock and now artfully arranged in a vase on the table. A butterfly had fluttered through the doorway and now reposed on one of the blossoms. Auriol made a ferocious swipe at it, caught it in her hand and crushed it. Nurse Murdock clinically reached for a paper napkin and handed it to Auriol who absent-mindedly took it and methodically wiped her hand clean. Laura had joined Fuller's group and said *sotto-voce*, 'I'm worried about Arthur. He's been behaving strangely from the moment he joined us at the airport. He didn't even react to the heliotrope.'

'What heliotrope?' asked Fuller.

'I was doused with it!' Laura said with exasperation. 'Elaine picked some up for me this morning!'

Fuller looked as though he was about to box her ears. 'That wasn't a very clever thing to do. The scent must have confirmed what he suspected we knew about him and Fiona and he's probably decided to take matters into his own hands. *Damn it!*' Laura didn't flinch. Fuller turned to Brian. 'Get the men in the village to arrange to have the car raised. They won't have the equipment here and will have to send to Wardsley for it.' Brian dispatched Aubrey Lewis to the village and he left at a half-trot. 'I'm going to the Welbecks to get Arthur.'

'I'm going with you,' stated Laura.

'You stay right here,' Fuller ordered, and Laura's chin

shot forward but she said nothing. Elaine Murdock was foraging in the refrigerator while Auriol helped herself to another brandy. The Vicar knew it was his duty to console Auriol but felt unenthusiastic. Edmund Kettering was dwelling on the late Viola and couldn't take his eyes from Laura. As Fuller headed for the door, he heard the sound of bicycle tires on the driveway gravel and a few seconds later one of the village constables, Andrew Kirby, appeared.

'Mr Fuller? Ah, there you are! Someone's fallen off the cliff at the hidden cove.' The room froze. 'It was seen from the *Atlantis* as it was sailing towards port. They weren't sure if it was a man or a woman. Sean Coleridge thought it might be a member of this household.'

'Where is he?' asked Fuller.

'Changing his clothes. He'll be along directly.'

Fuller turned to the Vicar. 'Could we use your car?'

'Mercy me yes!' cried the Vicar.

Fuller motioned to Brian and with the constable they ran to the Vicar's car. Laura stood at the window and watched them drive off.

'What have we done?' the Vicar asked dramatically. 'Are we under a *curse*?'

Auriol began wailing again, Ed Kettering crossed to her, Elaine Murdock bit into a stalk of celery and Laura slipped out the door.


Sean Coleridge, now decked out in tight blue jeans, white moccasins and a white turtle-neck pullover came rushing down the gangplank towards his two-seater. As he dashed passed his first mate, Billy Merkle caught a whiff of bay rum.

Sean's heart was pounding as he slipped behind the wheel, slammed the door shut, turned the key in the ignition and then drove off leaving Merkle enveloped in a cloud of dust. Coleridge crouched over the wheel as though a red flag had signalled him into the race of his lifetime. He could see the trophy awaiting him at the end of the run. He could see Laura standing there with laurel wreath out-stretched. Only one thing marred the effect. Both Laura and the laurel wreath were sopping wet.

Laura passed through the trees on the same path taken earlier by her husband. She paused upon encountering the statues and her mind reverted to her nightmare. *A white column,* and here stood five of them. She felt dizzy and put a hand on Sappho to steady herself. In a few moments, the dizziness passed and Laura was staring at the face that bore some resemblance to Fiona Cooper.

*Maybe it's the moon over Cornwall. . . .*

She was singing the words softly without realising it. Damned song, she thought with irritation, it'll probably haunt me for the rest of my life. Maybe it's the moon over Cornwall indeed! Soppy sentimental. . . . Maybe it's the moon over *what*?

She stood staring at the statue of Sappho with her mouth open.

*I recall the words!*

She drew her arms around her and stared at the Welbeck house.

I think I'm beginning to remember it *all*!

She directed her eyes from the house to the studio.

That night . . . that awful night . . . we were in the *studio* that night! Fiona and I were in the studio *that night*!

She realised she was trembling and pressed her hands to her cheeks to force the curtain surrounding her memory to rise further. Her hands lowered and she clenched her fists.

Frank will know why we came to the studio. He *has* to know. He'll tell me!

She was running towards the studio.

The constable seated alongside Fuller in the Vicar's car directed him to an old road that led to the hidden cove. The car bounced and suffered over rocks and ruts and Fuller finally pulled up at the cliff's edge. The men poured out of

180

the car and with the constable in lead, sprinted towards the edge.

The red blob was still visible under the rippling water, but a portion of it was obscured by a body sprawled face downward atop it.

'There's a path leading down there,' suggested Brian breathlessly.

'There's no need,' said Fuller. 'I can tell who it is.'

Shortly after Laura left the cottage, Elaine Murdock, her arms laden with packages of food designated for the over-due lunch, pushed the refrigerator door shut with her knee and noticed with dismay that Laura was no longer in the room. She hurried to the kitchen table, dumped her load and rushed to the door. In the distance, she saw Laura disappearing into the bordering trees and spoke to Ed Kettering with what sounded to him like an alarming urgency.

'Dr Kettering, I think Mrs Denning has gone to visit the Welbecks. Would you please go after her? Stay with her, don't let her out of your sight. Please hurry!' Ed Kettering rushed out the door in pursuit of Laura. The Vicar picked at a block of cheddar with his chubby fingers while Auriol attempted to focus her brandy-fogged eyes.

'Is it true, I'll never see my darling Fiona again? Must my last memory of her be a figure fleeing out the door with her maxicoat swirling about her feet?' She slapped the Vicar's hand. 'Use a knife! Fingers are unsanitary!' She stared up at Elaine Murdock. 'Who are you?'

'I'm Elaine Murdock. Mrs Denning's nurse.'

'Of course. You must be. You're wearing a uniform,' she said vaguely. 'Where is Laura?'

'She'll be back shortly,' said Nurse Murdock with her fingers crossed.

'And her memory . . . will that ever be the same again?'

'I think it already is.'

Laura tried the knob of the studio door, but it held firm.

'Frank! Frank?' she called out. 'Are you in there? It's Laura.' She brought a cheerful note to her voice. 'The prodigal's returned! Are you there, Frank? Aren't you glad I'm back?' She pressed her ear to the door and heard footsteps. She moved back as she heard the door being unbolted, and then slowly it began to swing open. She saw no one and took a step into the studio, pushing the door back with her left hand.

'Frank?' Her voice creaked like the door hinges.

'Frank?'

And then she saw the knife.

Fuller bore down on the accelerator as the car neared Laura's cottage. Through the windshield from the opposite direction, he saw Coleridge's two-seater pulling into Laura's driveway. The gathering of the clan, he thought to himself. That accounted for everyone involved in the case. No time will be wasted rounding them up. Laura the flame has drawn the moths. *I suppose you're wondering why I've asked you all here.* Brian was startled to hear Fuller chortling.

'That knife!' Laura said, stifling a scream.

Frank Welbeck emerged from behind the door. Laura stared into his face and fear seized her as she backed away from him. His face was contorted with maniacal hatred, his teeth bared like an animal about to spring.

'*Frank!*' Laura gasped and then a shocking, brutal blow on her back sent her sprawling forward.

'Sean! Sean!' wailed Auriol Kendall, 'Fiona is dead! She's been *murdered*!'

It was not the greeting Coleridge had looked forward to receiving on his arrival at the cottage. The news stunned him and paralysed his tongue. He could hear another car drive up and the sound of doors slamming, but he was too shocked to turn his head. Then he heard the nurse say, 'Clive! Laura's slipped away! She's gone to the Welbecks! I've sent Dr Kettering after her!'

'Damn!' Fuller shouted and Coleridge awakened. He spun on his heels and saw Clive Fuller racing across the field towards the trees with Cummings and the constable. Instinctively, Coleridge set out after them.

The Vicar, to his dismay, realised Auriol Kendall was gripping his right hand. 'Console me,' she pleaded, 'console me.'

'Ah! Ah so!' said the Vicar nervously, and then he puckered his face into what he hoped was a look of benevolence and said huskily, 'Auriol, why don't you eat something?'


Laura was frantically trying to get up as she heard the sound of a struggle behind her. A shout came from the doorway and she turned her head as Edmund Kettering came rushing in with a look of horror on his face. 'Frank!' he cried, 'Frank . . . *don't!*'

Laura saw Welbeck, right arm raised, holding what she thought was some sort of weapon, poised to plunge.

'*Frank!*' she screamed, 'No, Frank . . . *No!*'

Edmund Kettering threw himself at Welbeck and sent the sculptor off balance. He staggered backwards and fell against the statue of Charlotte Corday. It swayed lightly and the overhead light was reflected in the blade of the pearl-handled knife Charlotte Corday clutched in her right hand. Laura heard an unearthly shriek as she scrambled to her feet. She saw Ed Kettering fending off two-clawlike hands scratching at his face. Frank Welbeck now seemed to be embracing the statue, staring at the face. Through his lips passed an unearthly whisper, '*Medusa!*'

Clive Fuller came rushing in, absorbed the situation in one glance, and rushed to Kettering's assistance. Brian and the constable entered and saw Laura with her hand gently laid on Welbeck's trembling shoulder.

'Laura! Laura *darling*!'

Laura turned with a perplexed look on her face as she saw a masculine vision in the doorway wearing white moccasins, tight blue jeans and white turtle neck sweater. 'Oh!' she said as a flash of recall struck, 'it's Sean. Well just don't stand there like a sex symbol, help me. Frank's on the verge of collapse!' At Welbeck's feet lay the pair of shears he had dropped. Coleridge had a tight grip on the man as Laura diverted her attention to the struggling, shrieking creature held in the grip of Fuller and Brian Cummings.

'Frankie! *Frankie!* They're hurting me, Frankie!'

Laura crossed to the struggling woman and struck her hard on the face. 'Settle down, girl,' Laura snapped. 'Frankie was about to plunge those shears in your heart.'

The struggle abated slowly and Emaline Welbeck gave way to tears and began to sink to the floor. Fuller and Brian released their grip, satisfied Emaline would give them no further trouble, Fuller went to Laura and put his arm around her.

'You okay?' he asked.

'More or less. Why?'

'Arthur's dead.' She gripped his arm. 'I'm sorry. It was he who fell from the cliff.'

'The hell he did,' cackled Emaline. 'I *pushed* him!'

.

Chapter Sixteen

It took the combined efforts of Coleridge, Brian and the constable to restrain Frank Welbeck when he moved to attack his sister. Emaline meantime, with insane unconcern, was staring at the statue of Charlotte Corday clutching the pearl-handled knife.

'Oh, Frankie, how could you,' she whimpered. 'How could you.'

Charlotte Corday's face was a brilliant likeness of Emaline Welbeck. Frank's face shot forward with a sneer, 'Medusa! *Medusa!*' His struggles ceased and he hung his head. Laura brought him the orange crate and he sat down.

Fuller was towering over Emaline. 'I'd appreciate the truth, Miss Welbeck.' Laura could hardly stop herself from bursting into laughter at his formal manner. The situation was all too bizarre. Arthur was dead and she was ashamed at her absence of tears. Arthur the unloved sent hurtling into space to a watery grave, his final indignity. She lowered herself on to the crate, jostled Welbeck with her hip and he automatically made room for her. He took her hand and caressed it tenderly and found the courage to look into her eyes.

'Forgive us, Laura. Find it in your heart to forgive us. If I thought my feeble efforts to protect Emaline would plunge you into the hell you must have suffered, I would never have done it.'

'Shut up, *Frankie!*' screeched Emaline. 'Shut up or you'll never get that knighthood!'

Welbeck's eyes never left Laura's face. 'She's quite mad, you know. Quite mad. Did you know we're twins?' Laura bit her lip. 'Yes. Twins. She's the eldest, but I've always looked after her. I'm so ashamed, but God help me, I loved her dearly. I only cheated on her once.'

'Auriol Kendall,' said Laura.

'Oh,' said Welbeck, 'she's broken her silence about that, has she? Poor Auriol. Laura, do you remember that night at all?'

'Most of it now, yes.'

'You and Fiona came to the studio. It was raining. Fiona was in a terrible state. I'd asked you both to come and see the completed Charlotte.' He nodded his head slowly. 'We'd finished that afternoon. I wanted to be alone to do the finishing touches.' Fuller could see that Laura was beginning to recall the incident. 'You came over later that night. It was my best work. And Fiona began to cry. She

185

told us then she was pregnant. Emaline came through the door at that moment and in her own mad way, without waiting to hear a further explanation from Fiona, simply heard her say "I'm pregnant" and immediately assumed I was responsible. She had come from the kitchen and was holding one of the pearl-handled knives from the set you gave us last Christmas. . . .'

Fuller shot a glance at Laura.

'She went for Fiona but you and I held her back. Fiona fled and I shouted to you to run and you did, but Emaline broke away from me and beat you to the door brandishing the knife.' *The nightmare*, Laura was thinking, *the nightmare*. 'I struggled with Emaline and you made your escape. She tore away from me and pursued you, but I caught her and somehow managed to calm her, but I couldn't convince her I was not the father of that child. Late the next morning you phoned. Emaline answered but wouldn't let you speak to me.'

Laura was rubbing her head. 'I think it was to tell you about Arthur and Fiona.' Her face brightened and she looked at Fuller. 'Yes! That was it! But Emaline was still in a rage, my God she was cursing me out!'

'Was I ever!' Emaline cackled. 'And I still don't believe a word of it! That's why I came to the house! I stole out from the front and surprised the two of you preparing lunch! It was over in a second! You didn't even hear me come in! You were in the sitting room phoning Frankie again! I came into the kitchen from the side door and Fiona was fixing a salad. I said her name once, she turned around, she saw the knife and screamed and you came running in, but it was too late! Too late! I stuck it in her stomach and she fell back against the table! You screamed and ran for me but I plunged the knife again and Fiona clutched her heart and staggered towards the door, but I shoved you away and struck her again and again and she fell against the wall by the stove and then slid to the floor. You kept mumbling but it's Arthur, Arthur as though I'd

186

believe *that*!'

Laura sat tensely staring at the mad woman who was making jabs at the floor with her index finger as she continued speaking.

'Then you came towards me and you reached for a kitchen chair. I thought you were going to hit me with it, so I went for you with the knife! But you just stood there ... staring at me ... paralysed ... you were stiff ... and a thought came to me.' She chortled. 'I think quick you know. I've always had to think quick. I wiped the knife hilt clean, put it on the table, helped you on to the chair and I waved my hand back and forth in front of your eyes, but they didn't flicker. They didn't see a thing. And that's when Frankie came in. And I yelled "Oh, my God, Frankie, look what *Laura's done to Fiona*!"'

Welbeck groaned and looked away from his sister.

'Look what she's done! *Look!*' Emaline was pointing at Charlotte Corday. 'They were fighting, Frankie! Fiona told Laura Arthur was the father of her baby! And she killed her!'

'I believed it then,' said Welbeck hoarsely, 'I believed it. I've seen Laura's rages before. But I wanted to help her. I said Emmy we have to help her. We love Laura. Fiona's coat was draped over a chair. One of those long ones ...'

'A maxicoat,' said Fuller.

'I wrapped the body in it and Emaline and I carried it out. We put it in the car and Emaline kept babbling if they don't find the body they don't have a case and then she had this crazy idea.'

'You've said *enough*, Frankie!'

'Shut your face!' he snapped. 'I left Emaline behind to clean up and I drove off with the body.'

'Everything would have been *fine*,' screeched Emaline, 'if that damn Arthur hadn't walked in right then. So I had to explain the whole damn thing to him the way I told it to Frankie. And he bought it all right. The jealous wife, he bought it! I guess when I got to the kitchen earlier I tore

187

the phone off the wall. I don't remember much of that.'

'You did,' said Laura. 'I rushed to call the police but you hit me away and tore the phone loose.'

'I don't remember that at all,' she said, shaking her head sadly. 'But if you say so, dear.'

'You did ... dear.'

'You want the rest of it?'

'We'd be most grateful,' said Fuller and Emaline rewarded him with a coquettish wink.

'Well, Arthur picked up Laura and carried her into the sitting room and placed her on the couch. He asked me to stay with her while he went for Kettering. But I couldn't do that. I had to look after Frankie. And then, I don't know, it seemed so right at the time. I took the knife in a napkin, and I placed it in Laura's hand. I held her fingers tight until the grip took ... and then I went to help Frankie.'

'Why'd you kill Arthur?' Fuller asked.

'He had time to think. He began to suspect it was me, not Laura. He followed me out to the hidden cove. I went there to pick sea heath for you, Laura.' Laura almost thanked her but bit her tongue instead. 'He accused me and of course I laughed in his face. And then I said to him, you want to see Fiona's car? Look down behind you! And the damn fool did and I pushed him and over he went screaming and screaming and then I heard him yelling for his mother! His *mother*!' She threw back her head and laughed and for a moment Laura thought she knew what Emaline Welbeck must have looked like as a young girl. When the laughter subsided, she fixed Laura with a cold stare. 'He wanted to be a hero in your eyes. He wanted to bring me in and clear you thinking he'd win you back that way. If it's any consolation to you, he never loved Fiona, he only loved you. But he told me you were beginning to remember. Yes he told me that. So I figured you had to be next.' She said it as though she might have been choosing her team for a parlour game. 'But I knew Frankie suspected it was me who'd really done in Fiona. He wasn't talking to me. He wasn't

188

my Frankie anymore. I'd always thought there was something between him and Fiona. They had a fight at that cocktail party you gave for your mother-in-law, remember?'

'Yes,' said Laura.

Fuller turned to Frank Welbeck. 'You drove the car to the hidden cove, released the brake and sent it over.' Welbeck nodded. 'Well,' sighed Fuller to Laura, 'once we recover the body, that wraps it up!'

'Ha Ha Ha Ha Ha!' laughed Emaline, 'Ha ha ha ha ha!'

Welbeck reached for the shears at his feet, got a tight grip on them, and with the shears poised to strike, leapt to his feet.

'Frank!' cried Laura in terror, but Welbeck didn't mean the shears for Emaline as Laura had thought. He was hacking away at Charlotte Corday's face. The plaster of paris began to crack and then pieces began to fall away and Laura later remembered she couldn't stop screaming when the last of the plaster of paris crumbled and she saw a head and a face she recognised as Fiona Cooper.

Arthur Denning had been late in arriving at the airport that morning because he stopped en route at his solicitor to give him an envelope he wouldn't trust to the mail. It was the document he had been feverishly writing that previous evening. It was a full statement about his small part in the crime and his belief that Emaline Welbeck was the guilty party. The document was to be opened only in the event of his death and given to Detective-Inspector Clive Fuller.

That night, after Frank and Emaline Welbeck had been taken to the jail in Wardsley, Edmund Kettering arrived at Laura's cottage. Shamefacedly, he told her he'd thought for a while she might have pushed Viola overboard.

'I have an idea when Emaline makes her statement tomorrow,' said Fuller, 'she'll admit it was she who did it. It was Emaline who was the only eye-witness. It was she who told everyone Viola was clutching Laura's hand.'

Kettering was pale. 'I think when Viola was posing for Frank, Emaline thought they were having an affair.'

'Probably,' said Fuller.

Laura said nothing. She was remembering everything now quite vividly. Frank Welbeck might have insisted he was unfaithful to his sister only once, but she strongly suspected Emaline had been quite right. Frank had undoubtedly had a brief go at Viola.

Kettering cleared his throat and asked Fuller, 'Will Frank be told the truth about Fiona?'

'No!' shouted Laura. 'Dear God don't anyone ever. It would be too awful for him now. I've already spoken to Auriol and surprisingly enough she agrees with me. Let's leave it that way. Anyone for a martini?'

Sean Coleridge never found the opportunity to propose marriage to Laura. The way Clive Fuller took her in his arms after Welbeck hacked away at the statue told him he'd be wasting time and breath and he returned to his boat and got very drunk in solitude.

When Laura phoned the news of Arthur's death to Dame Marjorie Denning, her mother-in-law stifled a sob, told Laura they must both be brave and nodded as Laura solemnly concurred, and after hanging up the phone poured herself a large sherry. She took the glass back to the desk, phoned her press secretary who made appropriate sympathetic noises and then said he would immediately see to the funeral arrangements. Dame Marjorie next phoned her dressmaker and ordered a new black dress and promised to be in early the next morning for a fitting. She then spent five minutes staring at the photograph of herself and little Arthur and was amazed to realise she was still capable of tears. Several weeks later, she established the Arthur Denning Memorial Award for Aspiring Young Writers.

Many months later, Laura Denning wrote in her diary. *Hello Again!*

*Well, the new book's finished and Clive's read it and says it is undoubtedly my best. I've dedicated it to him which I can see pleases him enormously. He hasn't looked that pleased since I told him marriage for us was out, for the time being anyway, as I now remember everything, especially that I am hell to live with and I love Clive too much to lose him which would happen I'm sure if we were living together under the same roof. We do love each other very much which is why our affair continues to be so perfect. Elaine Murdock phoned to say she's pregnant and if it's a girl, she's going to call her Laura. Isn't that darling? Clive tells me poor old Emaline passed away after an apoplectic stroke which had left her in a cataleptic state and of course never realised the irony, and I still tremble at the memory of Frank's suicide, hari-kiri with one of the pearl-handled knives while out on bail. Harborford is peaceful and lovely again though we were all rather sorry to see Sean Coleridge sail away on the Atlantis for the South Seas. We've all recovered from the news that Auriol is to become Mrs Edmund Kettering and still don't understand why the Vicar got hysterical when Auriol asked him to perform the marriage.*

*Time for a fresh paragraph. Clive is driving up tonight and we'll probably have dinner at the Inn. I hope he likes the title I've finally selected for the new book, The Affair at Royalties.*